Kirk Munroe

Campmates

A Story of the Plains

Kirk Munroe

Campmates
A Story of the Plains

ISBN/EAN: 9783743398757

Manufactured in Europe, USA, Canada, Australia, Japa

Cover: Foto ©Andreas Hilbeck / pixelio.de

Manufactured and distributed by brebook publishing software (www.brebook.com)

Kirk Munroe

Campmates

CAMPMATES

A Story of the Plains

By
KIRK MUNROE

Author of
"THE FLAMINGO FEATHER" "WAKULLA" "DORYMATES"
"DERRICK STERLING" ETC.

Illustrated

HARPER & BROTHERS PUBLISHERS
NEW YORK AND LONDON

CONTENTS.

Contents.

ILLUSTRATIONS.

CAMPMATES.

A Story of the Plains.

CHAPTER I.

A WEARY RIDE.

SLOWLY and heavily the train rumbled on through the night. It was called an express; but the year was long ago, in the early days of railroading, and what was then an express would now be considered a very slow and poky sort of a train. On this particular night too, it ran more slowly than usual, because of the condition of the track. The season was such a wet one, that even the oldest traveller on the train declared he could not remember another like it. Rain, rain, rain, day after day, for weeks, had been the rule of that spring, until the earth was soaked like a great sponge. All the rivers had overflowed their banks, and all the smaller streams were raging torrents, red, yellow, brown, and sometimes milky white, according to the color of the clays through which they cut their riotous way. The lowlands and meadows were flooded, so that the last year's hay-stacks, rising from them here and there, were veritable islands of refuge for innumerable rabbits, rats, mice, and other small animals, driven by the waters from their homes.

And all this water had not helped the railroad one bit. In the cuts the clay or gravel banks were continually sliding down on the track; while on the fills they were as continually sliding out from under it. The section gangs were doubled, and along the whole line they were hard at work, by night as well as by day, only eating and sleeping by snatches, trying to keep the track in repair, and the road open for traffic. In spite of their vigilance and unceasing labor, however, the rains found plenty of chances to work their mischief undetected.

Many a time only the keen watchfulness of an engine-driver, or his assistant, the fireman, saved a train from dashing into some gravel heap, beneath which the rails were buried, or from plunging into some yawning opening from which a culvert or small bridge had been washed out. Nor with all this watchfulness did the trains always get through in safety. Sometimes a bit of track, that looked all right, would suddenly sink beneath the weight of a passing train

into a quagmire that had been formed beneath
it, and then would follow the pitiful scenes of a
railroad wreck.

So nobody travelled except those who were
compelled to do so, and the passenger business
of this particular road was lighter than it had
been since the opening. It was so light that on
this night there were not more than half a dozen
persons in the single passenger coach of the express, and only one of these was a woman. Another was her baby, a sturdy, wholesome-looking
little fellow, who, though he was but a year old,
appeared large enough to be nearly, if not quite,
two. He had great brown eyes, exactly like
those of his mother. She was young and pretty,
but just now she looked utterly worn out, and no
wonder. The train was twelve hours late; and,
instead of being comfortably established in a
hotel, at the end of her journey by rail, as she
had expected to be before dark that evening, she
was wearily trying to sleep in the same stuffy,
jolting car she had occupied all day and had no
hope of leaving before morning.

There were no sleeping-cars in those days, nor
vestibuled trains, nor even cars with stuffed easy-
chairs in which one could lie back and make
himself comfortable. No, indeed; there were no
such luxuries as these for those who travelled

by rail at that time. The passenger coaches were just long boxes, with low, almost flat roofs, like those of freight cars. Their windows were small, and generally stuck fast in their frames, so that they could not be opened. There was no other means of ventilation, except as one of the end doors was flung open, when there came such a rush of smoke and cinders and cold air that everybody was impatient to have it closed again.

At night the only light was given by three candles that burned inside of globes to protect them from being extinguished every time a door was opened. There were no electric lights, nor gas, nor even oil-lamps, for the cars of those days, only these feeble candles, placed one at each end, and one in the middle of the coach. But worst of all were the seats, which must have been invented by somebody who wished to discourage railroad riding. They were narrow, hard, straight-backed, and covered with shiny leather.

In a car of this description the young mother, with her baby, had travelled a whole day, and nearly a whole night. It is no wonder then that she looked worn out, or that the baby, who had been so jolly and happy as to be voted a remarkably fine child by all the passengers, should have sunk into an exhausted sleep, after a prolonged fit of screaming and crying, that caused the few remaining inmates of the car to look daggers at it, and say many unkind things, some of which even reached the ears of the mother.

During the day there had been other women in the car, travelling for shorter or longer distances. To one of these, a lady-like girl who occupied an adjoining seat for some hours, and who was greatly interested in the baby, the young mother had confided the fact that this was his birthday, and also part of her own history. From this it appeared that she was the wife of an army officer, who was stationed with his regiment in the far West. She had not seen him for nearly a year, or just after the baby was born; but at last he had been ordered to a fort on the upper Mississippi River, where he hoped to remain for some time. Now his young wife, who had only been waiting until he could give her any sort of a home with him, had bravely set forth with her baby to join him. He had written her that, on a certain date in the spring, a detachment of troops was to start from St. Louis by steamboat for the fort at which he was stationed. As one of the officers of this detachment was to take his wife with him, he thought it would be a fine opportunity for her to come at the same time. She wrote back that she could not possibly get ready by the date named, but would come by a later boat. After she had sent the letter, she found that she could get ready; and, as the aunt with whom she was living was about to break up her home and go abroad, she decided to start at once for St. Louis. There she would join her husband's friends, travel with them to the far-away fort, and give the lonely soldier a joyful surprise. There was no time to send another letter telling him of her change of plan, and she was glad of it, for a surprise would be so much nicer.

The early part of her journey had been accomplished quite easily. There had been no rains in the East, such as were deluging the whole Ohio valley. If there had been, it is not likely the soldier's wife would have undertaken to travel at that time, and expose her precious baby to such terrible risks, even to carry out the surprise she anticipated so joyfully. From her aunt's house, in New York city, she had travelled by steamer up the Hudson to Albany. From there she took cars to Buffalo, and a lake boat to Cleveland. Now she was travelling by rail again, across the flooded state of Ohio towards Cincinnati. There she intended taking a steamboat down the Ohio River, and up the Mississippi to St. Louis, where she expected to join her husband's friends, on the boat that would carry them all to their journey's end.

The details of this plan were fully discussed by the occupants of the adjoining seats in the car, and when it came time for the one who was not going through to leave the train, and take another at a small junction, she had become so greatly interested in her new acquaintance that she begged the latter to write to her, and tell her how she got along. She wrote her own name and address on a bit of paper, just before leaving the car, and gave it to the soldier's wife; but, in her hurry, neglected to make a note of the name given her in return, and afterwards, when she tried to recall it, was unable to do so.

The tediousness of the weary day had been so much lessened by the making of this pleasant acquaintance, that for some time after her departure the young mother remained light-hearted and cheerful. The baby, too, was bright and happy, and a source of constant amusement, not only to her, but to all those about him.

After a while, though, when it grew dark, and the feeble candles were lighted, and most of the passengers had left the car, and the baby at first fretted and then screamed, refusing to be quieted for more than an hour, the exhausted young mother grew nervous and frightened. Only the thought of the glad meeting, and the great happiness awaiting her at the end of this tedious journey, enabled her to bear it as bravely as she did.

At length the babe cried himself to sleep, and the tired arms that had held him so long gladly laid him down in a nest made of shawls and his own dainty blanket on the opposite seat. This blanket had the initials "G. E." embroidered in one corner, though these did not stand for the baby's name. In fact, he had no first name, nor had he yet been christened. This ceremony having been postponed until both the father and mother could take part in it; the question of a name had also been left undecided until then. The young mother wanted her boy called "Gerald," after his father, and she had even embroidered the inital "G." on his blanket to see how it would look. Thus far, however, the baby was only called "baby," and had no right to any other name.

As the child slept quietly in spite of the jar and jolt and rumble of the train, the fair young head of the mother who watched so fondly and patiently over him gradually drooped lower and lower. The brown eyes, so like the baby's, closed for longer and longer intervals, until at length she, too, was fast asleep, and dreaming of the joy that awaited her journey's end.

Chapter II.

A RUDE BAPTISM.

THERE were others on that train equally weary with the young mother, and even more anxious; for they knew better than she the ever-present dangers of that water-soaked road-bed, and they bore the weight of a fearful responsibility.

The conductor, looking grave and careworn, started nervously at every lurch of more than ordinary violence, and kept moving uneasily from end to end of his train. He never passed the young mother and her sleeping babe without casting sympathetic glances at them. He had done everything possible for their comfort, but it was little enough that he could do, and for their sake, more than anything else, he wished the trip were ended.

All through the long, dark hours, the brakemen stood on the platforms of the swaying cars, ready at a moment's warning to spring to the iron brake-wheels. This crew of train hands had only come on duty at nightfall, and had little knowledge of the through passengers.

In the locomotive cab, gazing ahead with strained eyes, were the engine-driver, Luke Matherson, and his fireman. Every now and then the latter found a change of occupation in flinging open the furnace door and tossing chunk after chunk of wood into the glowing interior. As he closed the door he would stand for a moment and look inquiringly at his companion, who sat motionless, with his hand on the throttle, and his eyes fixed steadily on the lines of track gleaming in the light of the powerful headlight. Occasionally, without turning his head, he exchanged a few words with the fireman.

"It's a nasty night, Luke," remarked the latter.

"Yes. It wouldn't take many more such to make me give up railroading."

"What do you think of the Beasely cut?"

"I'm afraid of it, and wish we were well through it."

"Well, we'll know all about it in five minutes more, and after that there's nothing serious but Glen Eddy creek."

The silence that followed was broken, a few minutes later, by two piercing blasts from the whistle. The fireman had already seen the danger, and sprung to the brake-wheel on the tender behind him. On every car the brakes were grinding harshly, set up by nervous, lusty young arms.

The train did not come to a standstill an instant too soon ; for, as it did so, the cow-catcher was already half buried in a slide from one of the treacherous banks of the Beasely cut.

An hour's hard work by all the train hands, and some of the passengers, with shovels and spades, cleared the track, and once more the express proceeded slowly on its uncertain way.

Now for the Glen Eddy bridge. Between it and the city that marked the end of the line was the best stretch of road-bed in the state. It was a long one, but it presented no dangers that a railroad man need fear.

The gray dawn was breaking as the train approached Glen Eddy creek. In the summer-time it was a quiet stream, slipping dreamily along between its heavily wooded banks. Now it was a furious torrent, swollen beyond all recognition, and clutching spitefully at the wooden piers of heavy crib-work that upheld the single span of the bridge.

The train was stopped and the bridge was examined. It seemed all right, and the conductor gave the word to go ahead. It was the last order he ever issued ; for, in another minute, the undermined piers had given way, and the train was piled up in the creek a shapeless wreck.

From that terrible plunge only two persons

escaped unharmed. One was Luke Matherson, the engine-driver, and the other was the baby. When the former felt his engine dropping from under him, he sprang from it, with desperate energy, far out into the muddy waters, that instantly closed over him. On coming to the surface, the instinct of self-preservation forced him to swim, but it was wildly and without an idea of direction or surroundings. For nearly a minute he swam with all his strength against the current, so that he was still near the wreck, when his senses were again quickened into action by a smothered cry, close at hand. At the same time a dark mass drifted towards him, and he seized hold of it. As the cry seemed to come from this, the man's struggles became directed by a definite purpose. Partially supporting himself by the wreckage, he attempted to guide it to the nearest bank ; but so swift was the current that he was swept down stream more than a mile before he succeeded in accomplishing his purpose.

Finally his feet touched bottom, and he drew his prize to shore. It was a car seat, torn from its fastenings. Tightly wedged between it and its hinged back was a confused bundle, from which came a smothered wailing. Tearing away the wrappings, Luke Matherson stared for a moment, in a dazed fashion, at what they had held so safely.

He could hardly believe that it was a live baby, lying there as rosy and unharmed as though in its cradle.

The sun had risen when the engine-driver, haggard, exhausted, with clothing torn and muddy, but holding the babe clasped tightly in his arms, staggered into the nearest farm-house, two miles back from the creek.

After his night of intense mental strain, the shock of the disaster, his plunge into the chilling waters, and his subsequent struggle to save the only surviving passenger of the train, it is not surprising that even Luke Matherson's strong frame yielded, and that for several weeks he was prostrated by a low fever. All this time the baby was kept at the farm-house with him, in order that he might be identified and claimed; but nobody came for him, nor were any inquiries made concerning the child. He was called "the Glen Eddy baby" by the few settlers of that sparsely populated region, who came to gaze at him curiously and pityingly. Thus those who cared for him gradually came to call him "Glen" for want of a better name; and, as the initials embroidered on the blanket saved with him were "G. E.," people soon forgot than Glen Eddy was not his real name.

Although several bodies were recovered from

the wreck of the express, that of the young mother was not among them ; and, as there was no one left alive who knew that she had been on the train, of course her death was not reported. Thus the mystery surrounding the Glen Eddy baby was so impenetrable that, after a while, people gave up trying to solve it, and finally it was almost forgotten.

When Luke Matherson recovered from his fever, nothing could induce him to return to his duties as engine-driver on the railroad.

" No," he said, " never will I put myself in the way of going through another such night as that last one."

He went to Cincinnati as soon as he was able to travel, and while there was offered a position in the engine-room of a large mill at Brimfield, in western Pennsylvania, which he accepted. The people of the farm-house where he had been ill were willing to keep the baby ; but Luke Matherson claimed it, and would not give it up.

The babe had been given to him, if ever one had, he said ; and, if no one else loved it, he did. Of course, if anybody could prove a better claim to it than his, he would be the last one to dispute it ; but, if not, he would keep the child and do the very best by him he knew how. He had no folks of his own in the world, and was only too glad to feel that one human being would grow up to care for him.

The farm-house people lost track of Luke Matherson when he left Cincinnati. Thus when, some four months later, a broken-hearted man, who had with infinite pains traced his wife and child to that line of railroad, reached that part of the country, he could gain no further information except that a baby, who might have been his, was saved from the Glen Eddy disaster, but what had become of it nobody knew.

CHAPTER III.

A BOY WITHOUT A BIRTHDAY.

"It's no use, Glen," said the principal of the Brimfield High School, kindly, but with real sorrow in his tone. "Your marks in everything except history are so far below the average that I cannot, with justice to the others, let you go on with the class any longer. So unless you can catch up during the vacation, I shall be obliged to drop you into the class below, and we'll go all over the same ground again next year. I'm very sorry. It is a bad thing for a boy of your age to lose a whole year; for this is one of the most important periods of your life. Still, if you won't study, you can't keep up with those who will, that's certain."

The boy to whom these words were spoken was a squarely built, manly-looking chap, with brown curling hair, and big brown eyes. He was supposed to be seventeen years old, but appeared younger. Now his cheeks were flushed, and a hard, almost defiant, expression had settled on his face.

"I know you are right, Mr. Meadows," he said, at length. "And you have been very kind to me. It's no use, though. I just hate to study. I'd rather work, and work hard at almost anything else, then I would know what I was doing; but as for grinding away at stupid things like Latin and geometry and trigonometry and natural philosophy, that can't ever be of any earthly use to a fellow who doesn't intend to be either a professor or an astronomer, I can't see the good of it at all."

"No, I don't suppose you can now," replied the principal, smiling, "but you will find even those things of use some time, no matter what you may become in after-life. I will try and talk with you again on this subject before I go away; but now I must leave you. I hope for your sake, though, that you will think better about studying, and not throw away your chance to do so now, while it is comparatively easy. To win success in life you must study some time, and if you had stood anywhere near as high as Binney Gibbs I might have managed to offer you—"

"Excuse me, Mr. Meadows, but I must speak with you just a moment," here interrupted a voice, and put an end to the conversation between the principal and the boy who had allowed his distaste for study to bring him into disgrace.

As he walked away from the school-house, carrying all his books with him, for the term was ended and the long vacation had begun, the flush of mortification, called to his cheeks by Mr. Meadows's remarks, still reddened them. He felt the disgrace of his position keenly, though he had told the other boys, and had tried to make himself believe, that he did not care whether he passed the examinations or not. Now that he had failed to pass, he found that he did care. What was it that Mr. Meadows might have offered him? It couldn't be *that*, of course; but if it should have been! Well, there was no use in crying over it now. Binney Gibbs had been honored, and he was disgraced. It was bad enough to realize that, without thinking of things to make it worse. He was thankful when he reached home and had closed the front door behind him; for it seemed as though everybody he met must know of his disgrace, and be smiling scornfully at him.

He was a sensitive chap, was this Glen Eddy; for that was his name, and he was the same one who, as a baby, was rescued by Luke Matherson from the railroad wreck so many years ago. Most people called him Glen Matherson, and on the school register his name was entered as Glen Eddy Matherson; but, ever since his last birthday, when Luke had told him that he was not his real father, and had fully explained their relations to each other, the boy had thought of himself only as Glen Eddy.

The master mechanic of the Brimfield Mills, for such Luke Matherson now was, had meant to keep the secret of the boy's life to himself, at least for some years longer. Glen had, however, heard rumors of it, and had on one occasion been taunted by an angry playmate with the sneer that he was only a nobody who didn't belong to anybody, anyhow.

Glen had promptly forced this tormentor to acknowledge that he did not know what he was talking about; but the taunt rankled all the same. A few days afterwards, which happened to be the one that was kept as his seventeenth birthday, he told his father of it, and asked what it meant.

Then Luke Matherson, greatly troubled, but seeing that the secret could not be kept any longer from the boy, told him what he knew of his history. He ended with, " It is fifteen years ago this very day, Glen, that the terrible wreck took place ; and, as you were then thought to be about two years old, I have called this your birthday ever since."

The boy was amazed and bewildered. No idea

that the one whom he had always called "father" was not such in reality had ever entered his head; but now that the truth was told him, it seemed strange that he had not always known it instinctively. He had known that Mrs. Matherson was not his own mother, for he was five years old when she assumed that position, and of course he had always known that the two children were not his own sisters, though he loved them as dearly as though they were. But now to find out that he did not really belong to anybody was hard.

Who were his real parents? Were they alive? Could he find them? were questions that now began to occupy the boy's mind most of the time.

One of the strangest things about this state of affairs was to discover that his birthday was not his birthday after all. It seemed as though some foundation on which he had rested in absolute trust of its security had suddenly been swept from under him, and left him struggling in a stormy sea of uncertainty.

The idea of a boy without a birthday! Who ever heard of such a thing? How the other fellows would stare and smile if they knew it! Glen had been so proud of his birthday, too, and it had been made so much of at home. His favorite dishes were always prepared for the meals of that day, his tastes were consulted in everything that was done, and his father always made a point of giving him a more valuable present then than even at Christmas. Why, on the last one, the very day on which the boy first learned how unreal the whole thing was, his father—no, his adopted father—had given him the dearest little silver watch that ever was seen.

Many times since learning such a sad lesson in the uncertainties of life, Glen had pulled this watch from his pocket, simply to assure himself of its reality, and that it was not a make-believe like his birthday.

But for his natural force of character and sweetness of disposition, Glen would have been a spoiled boy; for Luke Matherson had never been able, since the moment he first saw him lying helplessly on the floating car seat, to cross him in anything, or deny him whatever he asked if it lay in his power to grant it. With his own children Mr. Matherson was rather strict; but with the orphan lad who had shared with him the greatest peril of his life, he could not be.

Thus Glen had grown up to be somewhat impatient of restraint, and very much inclined to have his own way. He was also a brave, generous boy, and an acknowledged leader among his young companions. Was he not the best swimmer, the fastest runner, the most daring climber, and expert horseback-rider in Brimfield? Was he not captain of the baseball nine? and did not all the fellows admire him except one or two, who were so jealous of his popularity that they sought to detract from it?

One of those who were most envious of him was Binney Gibbs, son of the wealthy owner of the Brimfield Mills. He was taller than Glen, but was no match for him in anything that called for muscle or pluck. It was he who had flung the taunt of Glen's being a nobody at the boy. Binney had never been noted for his studious habits until both he and Glen entered the High School at the same time. Then, realizing that he could not excel at anything else, he determined to beat the other at his studies. To this end he strained every nerve with such effect that he not only outranked Glen in his own class, but, by working all through two long vacations, gained a whole year on him. So now, while poor Glen was threatened with being turned back from the second class, Binney Gibbs had just graduated at the head of the first, and was ready to enter college. And the worst of it all was that everybody believed him to be a whole year younger than Glen, too.

To be sure, Binney was pale and thin, and no

stronger than a cat. Why, he couldn't even swim; but what of it? Had he not beaten the most popular fellow in town away out of sight in this scholarship race? To crown his triumph another thing had happened to make Binney Gibbs the envy of all the boys in Brimfield, but particularly of Glen Eddy.

On that last day of school the diplomas had been awarded, and Binney's had been handed to him the first of all. As he was about to return to his seat, amid the loud applause of the spectators, Mr. Meadows asked him to wait a minute. So Binney stood on the platform while the principal told of a wonderful exploring expedition that was being fitted out at that moment, to go across the plains through the almost unknown territories of New Mexico and Arizona to California. It was to be the most famous expedition of the kind ever sent into the far West; and, as it was to be partly a government enterprise, all sorts of political influence was being used to obtain positions in it. It was to be commanded by a noted general, who was an old friend of Mr. Meadows.

"Now," said the principal, "the general writes that he will give a position in this party to the boy who stands highest in my school this year, or, if I cannot recommend him, or he does not choose to accept it, to any other whom I may name." Here Mr. Meadows was interrupted by prolonged applause.

When it had subsided, he continued. "There is no question as to which pupil of the school ranks highest this year. He stands before you now, with his well-earned diploma in his hand [applause], and it gives me great pleasure to be able to offer to Master Binney Gibbs a position in the exploring-party that will start from St. Louis two weeks from to-day, under command of my friend General Lyle. I hope that he may be induced to accept it, and that his parents may permit him to do so; for I cannot imagine a more fascinating or profitable way of spending a year at his time of life.

Chapter IV.

Mr. Meadows's remarks in regard to the famous exploring expedition, about to be sent across the Western plains, were received with tremendous applause, and Binney Gibbs at once became an object of envy to every boy in the school—to say nothing of the girls. What a chance to have offered one just for doing a little hard study! If the other boys had known of it, how they, too, would have studied! Binney Gibbs would have been obliged to work harder than he had for his position! Yes, sir! ten times harder!—only think of it! Indians and buffalo and bears, and the Rocky Mountains, and all the other enchanted marvels of that far-away region. Why, just to contemplate it was better than reading a dime novel!

While these thoughts were racing through the minds of his companions, and while they were cheering and clapping their hands, the lucky boy himself was talking with Mr. Meadows, and telling him how much he should like to join that expedition, and how he hoped his father would let him do so.

Mr. Gibbs left his seat in the audience and stepped up to the platform, where he talked for a moment with Mr. Meadows. Then he spoke to Binney, and then, as he faced the school, they saw that he had something to say to them.

It was that he was proud of his son—proud of the honor shown to the school and to Brimfield through him—and that he should certainly allow Binney to accept the offered position.

So it was settled; and all the boys cheered again. To Glen Eddy it seemed that he would be willing to forego all the other good things that life held for him if he could only have the prospect of one such year of adventure as was promised to Binney Gibbs. For the first time in his life he was genuinely envious of another boy.

It was that same day, after everybody else had gone, that he had the talk with Mr. Meadows, in which the latter told him he must go back a whole year on account of not having studied; though, if he had, he might have been offered— And then came the interruption. Glen was too heart-sick and miserable to wait and ask what the offer might have been. Besides, he thought he knew, and the thought only added to his distress of mind, until it really seemed as though no boy could be much more unhappy than he.

Mr. Matherson knew how the boy stood in school, for the principal had thought it his duty to inform him; and that evening he and Glen had a long and serious talk.

"It's no use, father; I just hate to study!" exclaimed Glen, using the same words that had caused Mr. Meadows to look grave earlier in the day.

"I fancy we all hate a great many things that we have to do in this life," replied the master mechanic, "and you have certainly had a strik·· ing example to-day of the value of study."

"Yes, that's so," admitted Glen, reluctantly, "and if I had known that there was anything of that kind to be gained, perhaps I might have tried for it too."

"If I had been given your chance to study when I was young," continued the other, "and had made the most of it, I would have a better position to-day than the one I now hold. As it is, I have had to study mighty hard, along with my work, to get even it. I tell you, my boy, the chances come when you least expect them. The only thing to do is to prepare for them, and be ready to seize them as they appear. If one isn't prepared they'll slip right past him—and when once they have done that, he can never catch them again."

"But aren't there working chances just as well as studying chances, father?"

"Of course there are, and the study must always be followed by work—hard work, too—but the first is a mighty big help to the other. Now I will gladly do all that I can to help you on with your studies, if you will study; but if you won't, you must go to work, for I can't afford to support you in idleness, and I wouldn't if I could."

"Well, I'll tell you what, father," said Glen, who was more inclined to take his own way than one proposed by somebody else, "if you can help me to the getting of a job, I'll try the work this summer, and when it comes time for school to open again, I'll decide whether it shall be work or study."

"All right, my boy, I'll do what I can to get you a place in the mill or in Deacon Brown's store, whichever you prefer."

Now that a definite kind of work was proposed, it did not seem so very desirable after all, and Glen doubted if he should like either the mill or the store. Still he did not say so, but asked for a day longer in which to decide, which was readily granted him.

At about the same time that evening, Binney Gibbs was saying to his father, with a self-satisfied air,

"Isn't it a good thing that I have stuck to my books as I have, and not wasted my time playing ball, or swimming, or doing the things that Glen Matherson and the other fellows seem to consider so important?"

"Well, yes," replied Mr. Gibbs, a little doubt-fully, "I suppose it is. At the same time, Binney, I do wish you were a little stronger. I'm afraid you'll find roughing it pretty hard."

"Oh, yes, I suppose physical strength was the most important thing when you were young, father; but nowadays its brain-work that tells," answered Binney, with a slight tone of contempt for his father's old-fashioned ideas. Binney was not a bad-hearted fellow—only spoiled.

The next day Glen did not feel like meeting any of his young companions. He wanted to think over the several problems that had been presented to him. So he wandered down to the river, where a fine new railroad-bridge, in the building of which he had been greatly interested, was now receiving its finishing touches. As he walked out towards the centre of the graceful structure, admiring, as he had a hundred times before, the details of its construction, its evident strength and airy lightness, he saw the engineer who had charge of the work standing, with a roll of plans under his arm, talking with one of the foremen.

Glen had visited the bridge so often that the engineer knew him by sight, and had even learned his name, though he had never spoken to him. He was, however, especially fond of boys, and had been much pleased with Glen's appearance. Several times he had been on the point of speaking to him, but had been restrained by the diffidence a man is so apt to feel in the presence of a stranger so much younger than himself. It is a fear that he may do or say something to excite the undisguised mirth or contempt that so often wait upon the ignorance of youth.

Without suspecting these feelings in him, Glen had been strangely attracted towards the engineer, whose profession and position seemed to him alike fascinating and desirable. He wished he could become acquainted with him, but did not know how to set about it. He, too, was diffident and fearful of appearing in an unfavorable light before the other, who was evidently so much older and wiser than he. But he did long to ask this engineer a great many questions.

Now he stood at a respectful distance and watched the young man, whose name he knew to be Hobart, and, wondering whether his position had been reached by study or work, wished he could think of some good excuse for speaking to him.

The floor of the bridge on which they were standing was about twenty-five feet above Brim River, the deep, swift stream that it spanned. Glen had swum and fished in it, and boated on it, until he knew its every current and slack-water pool. He knew it as well as he did the road to the village, and was almost as much at home in the one as on the other.

In order to consult a note-book that he drew from his pocket, Mr. Hobart laid his roll of plans on a floor-beam, at his feet, for a moment. Just then a little whirling gust of wind came along, and in an instant the valuable plans were sailing through the air towards the sparkling waters, that seemed to laugh at the prospect of bearing them away far beyond human reach.

The engineer tried in vain to clutch them as they rolled off the floor-beam, and uttered an exclamation of vexation as they eluded his grasp.

As he looked around to see what could be done towards their recovery, a boyish figure, without hat, jacket, or shoes, sprang past him, poised for an instant on the end of the floor-beam, and then leaped into space. Like a flash of light it shot downward, straight and rigid, with feet held tightly together, and hands pressed close against the thighs. A myriad of crystal-drops were flung high in the air and glittered in the bright sunlight as Glen, striking the water with the impetus of a twenty-five-foot fall, sank deep beneath its surface.

Chapter V.

SWIMMING INTO A FRIENDSHIP.

ALTHOUGH Glen found no difficulty in coming
to the surface, almost at the spot where the roll
of plans floated, and grasping it, he did not find
it so easy to bring it safely to shore. To begin
with, the roll occupied one hand, so that he had
but one for swimming. Then the current was
strong, and the banks steep. He was very near
the middle of the river. Any other Brimfield
boy would have been in despair at finding himself in such a situation. But, then, no other boy
in Brimfield would have taken that leap.

For a moment Glen wondered what he should
do. Then he remembered the " back-set " at the
Bend, a quarter of a mile below the bridge. It
would put him right in to the bank, at a place
where it was low, too. The anxious watchers on
the bridge wondered to see the boy turn on his
back and quietly drift away with the current,
at the same time holding the roll of plans, for
which he had dared so much, clear of the water.

They shouted to him to swim towards one or

the other bank and they would fling him a rope; but Glen only smiled without wasting any breath in answering. Most of the men ran to one end of the bridge, because it looked to them as though the boy were nearer that bank than the other; but Mr. Hobart, who had studied the river, remembered the Bend, and hurried to the other end. When he reached it he ran down along the bank, towards the place where he felt certain the boy would attempt to land. He got there in time to see Glen swimming with all his might to get out of the main current and into the "back-set." With two hands he would have done it easily; but with only one it was hard work. Then, too, his clothing dragged heavily.

Mr. Hobart shouted to him to let go the roll. "Drop it and make sure of your own safety," he cried. "They are not worth taking any risks for." But Glen was not the kind of a boy to let go of a thing that he had once made up his mind to hold on to, so long as he had an ounce of strength left.

So he struggled on, and at last had the satisfaction of feeling that something stronger than his own efforts was carrying him towards shore. He had gained the "back-set," and, though its direction was rather up along the bank, than in towards it, the swimmer had still strength enough left to overcome this difficulty.

A tree, growing straight out from the bank, overhung the stream, so that Glen at length drifted under it, and caught hold of a drooping branch. He had not strength enough to pull himself up; but it was not needed. With the activity that comes from a life spent in the open air, the engineer had run out on the horizontal trunk, and now, lying flat on it, he could just reach the boy's hand. In another minute the strong arms had drawn Glen up to a secure resting-place, where he might regain his breath and drip to his heart's content.

"Here are the plans, Mr. Hobart," he said, shyly, and at the same time proudly. "I hope they are not spoiled by the water. I held them out of it as much as I could."

"I hope you are not spoiled by the water, Glen Matherson," laughed the engineer, as he took the wet roll from the boy's hand. "You have done splendidly, and I am sincerely grateful to you for rescuing my plans, which are indeed of great value. At the same time I wouldn't do such a thing again, if I were you, for anything less important than the saving of life. It was a big risk to take, and I should have suffered a life-long sorrow if anything had gone wrong with you."

Although it was a warm June day, and Glen

laughed at the idea of catching cold, he had been in the water long enough to be thoroughly chilled. So, when they regained the bank, Mr. Hobart insisted that he should take off his clothes, wring them, and let them dry in the hot sun. In the meantime a workman had come down from the bridge with the boy's hat, jacket, and shoes. He lent him his overalls, and, thus comically arrayed, Glen sat and talked with the engineer while his clothes were drying.

How kindly the brown-bearded face was, and with what interest the man listened to all the boy had to say. How pleasant was his voice, and, in spite of his age (he was about thirty-five) and wisdom, how easy it was to talk to him! It was so easy, and he proved such a sympathetic listener, that before Glen knew it he found himself confiding all his troubles and hopes and perplexities to this new friend. It began with his name, which he told the engineer was not Matherson, and then he had to explain why it was not.

Then they wondered together what sort of a man Glen's real father could be, provided he were alive; and if, by any strange chance, he and his son would ever meet and know each other. Mr. Hobart did not think it at all likely they ever would. From this the boy was led to tell of his dislike for study, and into what trouble it had led him. He even told of the decision reached by his adopted father and himself the evening before, and the undesirable choice of work that had been presented to him.

"And so you don't think you would fancy either the mill or the store?" asked Mr. Hobart.

"No, sir, I do not. Each one, when I think of it, seems worse than the other, and they both seem worse than most anything else."

"Worse than studying?"

"Just as bad, because either of them means being shut up, and I hate to stay in the house. I should like some business that would keep me out-of-doors all the time."

"Ploughing, for instance, or driving a horse-car, or digging clams, or civil-engineering, or something nice and easy, like any of those?" suggested Mr. Hobart, gravely.

"Civil-engineering is what I think I should like better than anything else in the world!" exclaimed the boy, eagerly. "That's what you are, isn't it, sir?"

"That is what I am trying to be," answered Mr. Hobart, smiling; and if, by years of hard work, hard study, and unceasing effort, I can reach a generally recognized position as an engineer, I shall be satisfied with my life's work."

"Do you have to study?" asked Glen, in amazement.

"Indeed 1 do," was the answer. "I have to study continually, and fully as hard as any school-boy of your acquaintance."

Glen looked incredulous. It is hard for a boy to realize that his school is only the place where he is taught how to study, and that his most important lessons will have to be learned after he leaves it.

"I think I should like to be a civil-engineer, anyhow," he remarked, after a thoughtful pause, because it is an out-of-door business."

"Yes," admitted the other, "it is to a great extent."

Then they found that Glen's clothing was dry enough to be worn, and also that it was dinner-time. So, after Mr. Hobart had shaken hands with the boy, and said he hoped to see him again before long, they separated.

That afternoon Glen, still wearing a perplexed expression on his usually merry face, walked down to the mill and looked in at its open door. It was so hot and dusty and noisy that he did not care to stay there very long. He had been familiar with it all his life; but never before had it struck him as such an unpleasant place to work in, day after day, month after month, and even year after year, as it did now. How hard people did have to work, anyway! He had never realized it before. Still, working in a mill must be a little harder than anything else. At any rate, he certainly would not choose to earn his living there.

Then he walked down to Deacon Brown's store. The deacon did a large retail business; this was a busy afternoon, and the place was filled with customers. How tired the clerks looked, and what pale faces they had. How people bothered them with questions, and called on them to attend to half a dozen things at once. How close and stuffy the air of the store was. It was almost as bad as that of the mill. Then, too, the store was kept open hours after the mill had shut down; for its evening trade was generally very brisk. It did not seem half so attractive a place to Glen now as it had at other times, when he had visited it solely with a view of making some small purchase. Perhaps going to school, and keeping up with one's class, was not the hardest thing in the world after all.

So the poor boy returned home, more perplexed as to what he should do than ever, and he actually dreaded the after-supper talk with his adopted father that he usually enjoyed so much.

When the time came, and Mr. Matherson asked, kindly, "Well, my boy, what have you decided to do?" Glen was obliged to confess that he was just as far from a decision as he had been the evening before.

Chapter VI.

RECEIVING AN OFFER AND ACCEPTING IT.

"Well, that is bad," said the master mechanic, when Glen told him that he had been unable to arrive at any decision in regard to going to work. "It is bad, for I can't see that there is anything open to you just now, except one of the two things we talked about last evening. At the same time, I hate to compel you, or even persuade you, to do anything that is hard and distasteful. If you were a year younger, I should say, 'Spend your vacation as you always have done, and have as good a time as you know how, without worrying about the future.' At seventeen, though, a boy should begin to look ahead, and take some decisive step in the direction of his future career. If he decides to study, he should also decide what he wants to study for. If he decides to work, he should have some object to work for, and should turn all his energies in that direction. I declare, Glen, I hardly know how to advise you in this matter. Do you think of any particular thing you would rather do, or try to be? If so, and I can help you to it, you know how gladly I will, in every way that lies in my power."

"It seems to me I would rather be a civil-engineer than anything else," answered the boy, a little hesitatingly.

"A civil-engineer!" exclaimed the other, in surprise; "why, Glen, lad, don't you know that it takes the hardest kind of study to be that?"

Just then their conversation was interrupted by the arrival of a visitor, who, to Glen's surprise, was none other than Mr. Hobart, the engineer whose position he had been thinking of as one of the most desirable in the world.

After a few moments' pleasant chat the visitor asked Mr. Matherson if he could have a private business talk with him. So Glen left the room, and wandered restlessly about the house, filled with a lively curiosity as to what business the engineer could have with his adopted father.

In the meantime Mr. Hobart was saying, "I have known your son for some time by sight, Mr. Matherson, and took a fancy to him from the first. We only got acquainted to-day, when he performed an act of daring in my presence, and at the same time rendered me an important service. I find him to be exactly such a boy as I supposed he was; a generous-hearted, manly

fellow, who is just now unhappy and discontent-
ed because he has no particular aim in life, and
does not know what he wants to do."

"Yes," said Mr. Matherson, "that is just the
trouble; and the worst of it is that I don't know
what to advise him."

"Then, perhaps, I am just in time to help you.
My work here is about finished, and in a few
days I am to leave for Kansas, where I am to
take charge of a locating-party on one of the Pacific railroads. If you are willing to let Glen go
with me, I can make a place for him in this party.
The pay will only be thirty dollars per month,
besides his expenses; but, by the end of the summer, I believe he will have gained more valuable
knowledge and experience than he could in a
year of home and school life. I believe, too,
in that time I can show him the value of an
education and the necessity of studying for it.
Now, without really knowing anything about it,
he thinks he would like to become a civil-engineer. After a few months' experience in the unsettled country to which I am going he will have
seen the rough side of the life, and can decide
intelligently whether he desires to continue in
it or not."

Mr. Matherson could hardly restrain his delight
at the prospect of such an opening for the boy

whom he loved so dearly; but he was too honest
to let him start out under false colors; so he
said,

"I can never tell you how grateful I am for
this offer, sir; but I don't want you to think that
my boy is any better than he really is. He is
not a good scholar, and seems to lack applica-
tion. Even now he is in danger of being turned
back a whole year in school because he has failed
to keep up with his class."

"I know all that," replied Mr. Hobart, smiling; "and it is one of the reasons why I want
him to go with me. I was very much such a
boy myself, and think I understand his state of
mind perfectly. He has reached the most trying period of his life, and the one where he most
needs encouragement and help. He has a sufficiently good education to build on, and is bright
enough to comprehend things that are clearly
explained to him. As for his having no knowledge of the peculiar studies necessary for an engineer, I am glad that he hasn't. I believe that
it is better for all boys to gain some practical
knowledge of the business they intend to follow
before they really begin to study for it. A few
months or a year of practice shows them in what
they are deficient and what they need to learn.
I could get plenty of young fellows to go out to

Kansas with me who are crammed with theoretical knowledge of surveying and engineering, but who are ignorant of its practice. Such chaps think they know it all, and are impatient of criticism or advice. I can get along better with one who knows little or nothing to begin with, but who is bright and willing to learn. In the end I will guarantee to make such a one the more valuable engineer of the two."

"It is a new idea to me," said Mr. Matherson, reflectively, "but I believe you are right."

"There is another reason why I fancy your boy, and think I can make an engineer of him," continued Mr. Hobart. "His physical condition seems to me to be perfect. As they say of prize animals, he seems to be sound in wind and limb, and without a blemish. Now, the life of an engineer, particularly in unsettled countries, is a hard one. He is exposed to all sorts of weather; must often sleep without a shelter of any kind, and must work hard from early dawn until late at night, sometimes on a scanty allowance of food. It is as hard as, and in many cases harder than, active service in the army. It is no life for weaklings, and we do not want them; but, from what I have seen of your boy, I do not believe that even you can point out any physical defect in his make-up."

"No, I certainly cannot," replied Mr. Matherson, heartily, glad of a chance to praise his boy without qualification, in at least one respect. "I believe him to be physically perfect, and I know that there is not a boy of his age in town who is his match in strength, agility, or daring."

"So you see," laughed the engineer, "he is exactly the boy I want; and if you will let him go with me I shall consider that you have conferred a favor."

"Of course I will let him go, sir, and shall feel forever grateful to you for the offer."

Thus it was all settled, and Glen was summoned to hear the result of the few minutes' conversation by which the whole course of his life was to be changed. By it, too, he was to be lifted in a moment from the depths of despondency and uncertainty to such a height of happiness as he had not dared dream of, much less hope for. The moment he entered the room he was assured, by the smiling faces of its occupants, that their topic of conversation had been a pleasant one; but when its nature was explained to him he could hardly credit his senses.

Would he like to go out to Kansas for the summer?—to a land still occupied by wild Indians and buffalo? The idea of asking him such a question! There was nothing in the whole

world he would like better!   Why, it was almost
as good as the position offered to Binney Gibbs;
and, certainly, no boy could ever hope for anything more splendid than that.   In two respects
he considered himself even more fortunate than
Binney.   One was that he was to go with Mr.
Hobart, whom he had come to regard with an
intense admiration as one of the wisest and kind-
est of men.   The other was that they were to
start on the third day from that time, while Binney would not go for nearly two weeks yet.

What busy days the next two were!   How
Glen did fly around with his preparations!   How
interested Mr. Hobart was, and how he laughed
at many of the excited boy's questions!   Ought
he to have a buckskin suit and a broad-brimmed
hat?   Should he need any other weapons besides a revolver and a bowie-knife?   Would it be
better to take long-legged leather boots or rub-
ber-boots, or both?   How large a trunk ought
he to have?

His outfit, prepared by Mr. Hobart's advice,
finally consisted of two pairs of double blankets,
rolled up in a rubber sheet and securely corded,
two pairs of easy, laced walking-shoes, and one
pair of leather leggings, three flannel shirts, three
suits of under-clothing, and six pairs of socks,
one warm coat, two pairs of trousers, a soft, gray

felt hat, half a dozen silk handkerchiefs, and the same number of towels. Of these he would wear, from the start, the hat, coat, one of the flannel shirts, one of the two pairs of trousers, a suit of underclothing, one of the silk handkerchiefs knotted about his neck, and one of the pairs of shoes. All the rest could easily be got into a small leathern valise, which would be as much of a trunk as he would be allowed to carry.

He would need a stout leather belt, to which should be slung a good revolver in a holster, a common sheath-knife, that need not cost more than thirty cents, and a small tin cup that could be bought for five.

Besides these things, Mrs. Matherson, who loved the boy as though he were her own, tucked into the valise a small case of sewing materials, a brush, comb, cake of soap, tooth-brush, handglass, and a Testament in which his name was written.

On the very day of his departure his adopted father presented the delighted boy with a light rifle of the very latest pattern. It was, of course, a breech-loader, and carried six extra cartridges in its magazine. In its neat canvas-case, Glen thought it was the very handsomest weapon he had ever seen, and the other boys thought so too.

With them he was the hero of the hour, and

even Binney Gibbs's glittering prospects were almost forgotten, for the time being, in this more immediate excitement.

Of course they all gathered at the railway station to see him start on the morning of the appointed day. It seemed as though almost everybody else in the village was there, too. Binney Gibbs was among the very few of Glen's acquaintances who did not come. So, amid tears and laughter, good wishes and loud cheerings, the train rolled away, bearing Glen Eddy from the only home he had ever known towards the exciting scenes of the new life that awaited him in the far West.

Chapter VII.

ACROSS THE MISSISSIPPI.

NEVER before, since he was first carried to Brimfield as a baby, had Glen been away from there; so, from the very outset, the journey on which he had now started, in company with Mr. Hobart, was a wonderful one. In school, besides history, he had enjoyed the study of geography, being especially fond of poring over maps and tracing out imaginary journeys. In this way he had gained a fair idea of the route Mr. Hobart and he were to pursue, as well as of the cities and other places of interest they were to see. There was one place, however, for which he was not prepared. It was early in the first night of the journey, and the boy had just fallen into a doze in his sleeping-car berth. As the night was warm, and there was no dust, the car door was open, and through it came a sudden shout of "Glen Eddy! Glen Eddy!"

As Glen started up, wide awake, and answering "Here I am," the train rumbled over a bridge. Then it stopped, and the meaning of the shout flashed into the boy's mind. He was at the very place where, so long ago, he had lost a father or mother, or both. All the details of that awful scene, as described by his adopted father, appeared vividly before him, and he seemed to see, through a gray dawn, the mass of splintered wreckage nearly covered by angry waters, the floating car seat with its tiny human burden, and the brave swimmer directing it towards land.

The train stopped but a moment, and then moved on. As it did so, Glen, who was in an upper berth, heard a deep sigh, that sounded almost like a groan, coming apparently from a lower berth on the opposite side of the car. Directly afterwards he heard a low voice ask, respectfully, " What is it, Governor? Are you in pain? Can I do anything ?"

" Nothing, Price, thank you. I had a sort of nightmare, that's all," was the reply, and then all was again quiet.

Glen wished he might catch a glimpse of the person who spoke last, for he had never seen a governor, and wondered in what way he would look different from other men. He would try and see him in the morning. Thus thinking, he fell asleep.

The next morning he was awakened by **Mr.** Hobart, and told to dress as quickly as possible, for they were within a few miles of East St. Louis, and would soon cross the Mississippi. This news drove all other thoughts from the boy's mind, and he hurried through his toilet, full of excitement at the prospect of seeing the mightiest of American rivers.

There was no bridge across the Mississippi then, either at St. Louis or elsewhere. Great four-horse transfer coaches from the several hotels were waiting for passengers beside the train where it stopped, and these were borne to the opposite bank by a steam ferry-boat with a peculiar name and of peculiar construction. The *Cahokia* looked like a regular river steamer, except that she had no visible paddle-wheels, not even one behind, like a wheelbarrow, as some of the very shoal-draught boats had. For some time Glen could not discover what made her go, though go she certainly did, moving swiftly and easily across the broad expanse of tawny waters towards the smoky city on its farther bank. He would not ask Mr. Hobart, for he loved to puzzle things out for himself if he possibly could. At length he discovered that the boat was double-hulled, and that its single paddle-wheel was located between the two hulls. Glen was obliged to ask the object of tnis; but when he was told that it was to protect the wheel from the great ice-cakes that floated down the river in winter, he wondered that he had not thought of that himself.

So he forgot to look for his governor, or ask about him until they reached the hotel where they were to get breakfast and spend a few hours. Then he was told that the person in whom he was interested was probably General Elting, who had just completed a term of office as governor of one of the territories, and who was now acting as treasurer of the very railroad company for which he was to work.

Glen regretted not having seen the ex-governor, but quickly forgot his slight disappointment in the more novel and interesting things that now attracted his attention. He had never been in a city before, and was very glad of a few hours in which to see the sights of this one; for the train that was to carry them to Kansas City would not leave until afternoon.

As the offices of the company by whom Mr. Hobart was employed were in St. Louis, he was obliged to spend all his time in them, and could not go about with Glen. So, only charging him to be on hand in time for the train, the engineer left the boy to his own devices.

Glen spent most of his time on the broad levee at the river's edge, where he was fascinated by the great steamboats, with their lofty pilot-houses, tall chimneys, roaring furnaces, and crews of shouting negroes, that continually came and went.

This seemed to be their grand meeting-point. On huge placards, swung above their gang-planks, Glen read that some of them were bound for New Orleans and all intermediate ports. Then there were boats for the Red, Arkansas, Yazoo, Ohio, Illinois, Missouri, and a dozen other rivers, tributary to the great Father of Waters. Still others were bound for Northern ports, even as far as distant St. Paul, in Minnesota.

Two o'clock found the boy at the railway station, standing beside the car in which all his belongings were already safely deposited, waiting anxiously for Mr. Hobart. Just as the train was about to start, that gentleman rushed into the station.

" Jump aboard, Glen," he said, hurriedly, "and go on to Kansas City with the baggage. Here is your pass and a note to Mr. Brackett. Report to him at the Kaw House. I am detained here by business, but will join you to-morrow or next day. Good-bye."

The train was already in motion, and in another moment the boy had lost sight of his only friend in that part of the world, and was whirling away towards an unknown destination. He felt rather lonely and forlorn at thus being cast upon his own resources, but at the same time he felt proud of the confidence reposed in him, and glad of an opportunity to prove how well he could take care of himself.

For several hours he was interested in watching the rapidly changing features of the landscape; but after a while he grew weary of this, and began to study his fellow-passengers. There were not many in the sleeper, and the only ones near him in whom he took an interest were a little girl, five or six years old, who was running up and down the aisle, and a lady, evidently the child's mother, who sat opposite to him. As he watched the little one she tripped and would have fallen had he not sprung forward and caught her. The child smiled at him, the mother thanked him, and in a few minutes he found himself playing with the former and amusing himself in entertaining her.

She told him that her name was Nettie Winn; but that her papa, who lived a long way off, and whom she was going to see, called her "Nettle." She was a bright, sunny-haired little thing, who evidently regarded elder people as having been created especially for her amusement and to obey her orders. As, in obedience to one of these, the boy carried her in his arms to the forward end of the car that she might look out of the window in the door, a fine-looking middle-aged gentleman spoke to him, remarking that he seemed very fond of children.

"Yes, sir, I am," answered Glen, "for I have two little sisters at home."

They exchanged a few more words, and Glen was so attracted by the stranger's appearance and manner that after the tired child had gone to sleep with her head in her mother's lap, he again walked to the end of the car in hopes that the gentleman might be inclined to renew their conversation. Nor was he disappointed; for the stranger welcomed him with a smile, made room on the seat beside him, and they were soon engaged in a pleasant chat.

It is not hard for a man of tact to win the confidence of a boy, so that, before long, the gentleman knew that this was Glen's first journey from home, and that he was going to Kansas to learn to be an engineer.

"Do you mean a civil-engineer?" he asked, "or an engine-driver?"

"Oh, a civil-engineer, of course!" answered the boy; "for I can run a locomotive now, almost as well as father, and that used to be his business."

Then he explained that his father, who was now a master mechanic, had given him careful instruction in the art of running a pony switch engine that belonged to the Brimfield Mills, and that once, when the engine-driver was ill, he had been placed in charge of it for a whole day.

"That is a most useful accomplishment," remarked the gentleman, "and one that I should be glad to acquire myself."

When the train stopped at an eating station they went in to supper together, and Glen began to think that, in his new friend, he had found a second Mr. Hobart, which was the very nicest thing he could think about anybody.

The boy did not forget to carry a cup of tea and a glass of milk into the car for Mrs. Winn and Nettie, for which act of thoughtfulness he was rewarded by a grateful smile and hearty thanks.

He wondered somewhat at the several men who every now and then came into the car and exchanged a few words in low tone with his other train acquaintance, and also wondered that the gentleman should leave the car and walk towards the forward end of the train every time it stopped at a station.

Glen was so tired that he had his berth made up and turned in very early ; but for a long time found himself unable to sleep, so busy were his thoughts. At length, however, he fell into a sound, dreamless slumber, that lasted for hours, though he knew nothing of the passage of time.

He was suddenly awakened by a loud noise, and found himself sitting bolt upright in his berth, listening, bewildered and half frightened, to a confused sound of pistol-shots, shouts, and screams. The train was motionless. The screams were evidently those of fright, and came from the car he was in, while the other and more terrifying sounds reached his ears from some distance.

Chapter VIII.

Springing from his berth, Glen began hastily to put on his shoes and the few articles of clothing he had laid aside. Several other passengers were doing the same thing, and each was asking the others what had happened; but nobody knew. All the alarming sounds had now ceased, even the women who had screamed being quiet, in the hope of discovering the cause of their terror.

Glen was the first to leave the car, and, seeing a confused movement of lanterns at the forward end of the train, he began to run in that direction. It was still dark, though there were signs of dawn in the sky. The train was not stopped at a station, but in a thick woods. As the boy reached the baggage-car, he was horrified to see that several men were lifting a limp and apparently lifeless body into it. The sight made him feel sick and faint. He stood for a moment irresolute. Then, two men, one of whom carried a lantern, came rapidly towards him.

"Here he is, now!" exclaimed one of them, as the light from the lantern fell on the boy's face. Glen recognized the voice. It was that of his recent acquaintance. Now he was coatless and bare-headed. In his hand was a Colt's revolver. The other man was the conductor of the train.

"This gentleman says you can run a locomotive. Is that so?" asked the conductor, holding up his lantern and scanning Glen's face keenly.

"Yes," answered the boy, "I can."

"Well, it looks like taking an awful risk to trust a boy as young as you; but I don't know what else we can do. Our engineer has just been killed, and the fireman is badly wounded. Two more men are hurt, and we've got to get them to a doctor as quick as we can. It's fifty miles to Kansas City, and there's only one telegraph station between here and there. It's ten miles ahead. We'll stop there, and send a despatch. Will you undertake to run us in?"

"Let me look at the engine first, and then I'll tell you," answered Glen, his voice trembling with excitement in spite of his efforts to appear calm.

The three went to the panting locomotive and swung themselves up into its cab. Glen shuddered as he thought of the tragedy just enacted in that cab, and almost drew back as he entered it. Then, controlling himself by a determined effort, he gauged the water, tested the steam, threw the lever over and back, opened the furnace door, glanced at the amount of fuel in the tender, and did it all with such a business-like air and appearance of knowing what he was about as to inspire both the men, who were watching him closely, with confidence.

"Yes," he said at length, "I'll take her in; but we shall need some more water."

"Good for you, son!" cried the conductor. "You're a trump! and I for one believe you'll do it."

"So do I," said the passenger; "and I'm thankful we've got such a plucky young engine-driver along."

"But who will fire?" asked Glen, hardly hearing these remarks, though, at the same time, sufficiently conscious of them to feel gratified that he had inspired such confidence.

"I will," replied the passenger, promptly.

"You, general!" cried the conductor in astonishment.

"Certainly! Why not I as well as another?"

"Very well," responded the conductor, "I'm only too glad to have you do it, if you will; then let us be off at once." And, springing to the ground, he shouted, "All aboard! Hurry up, gentlemen, we are about to move on."

But Glen would not start until he had taken a flaring torch and the engine-driver's long-nosed oil-can, and walked all around the locomotive, examining every part of the huge machine, pouring on a little oil here and there, and making sure that everything was in perfect working order.

Then he again swung himself into the cab, pulled the whistle lever for one short, sharp blast, opened the throttle slowly, and the train was once more in motion.

It had hardly gone a hundred yards before two rifle-shots rang out of the forest, and one ball crashed through both windows of the cab, but without harming its occupants. Glen started; but his hand did not leave the throttle, nor did his gaze swerve for an instant from the line of gleaming track ahead. He had no time then to think of his own safety. He was too busy thinking of the safety of those so suddenly and unexpectedly intrusted to him.

The new fireman glanced at him admiringly, and murmured to himself, "That boy is made of clear grit. I would that I had a son like him."

This man, who was heaving great chunks of wood into the roaring furnace with the strength and ease of a trained athlete, formed no unpleasant picture to look upon himself. He was tall and straight, with a keen, resolute face, an iron-gray, military moustache, and close-cropped hair. He looked not only like a soldier, but like one well accustomed to command. At the same time he obeyed promptly, and without question, every order issued by the young engine-driver on the opposite side of the cab.

As the train dashed along at full speed there was no chance for conversation between the two, even had they felt inclined for it. Both were too fully engaged in peering ahead along the un-familiar line of track to pay attention to aught else.

Presently the conductor clambered over the tender from the baggage-car, and stood in the cab with them, to post Glen as to the grades and crossings.

It lacked a few seconds of fifteen minutes from the time of their starting, when they slowed down for the telegraph-station, the lights of which were twinkling just ahead. Here, while the conductor roused the operator, and sent his despatch, the locomotive was run up to the tank, and a fresh supply of water was taken aboard.

Then they were off again—this time for a run of forty miles without a stop or check. Day-light was coming on so rapidly now that the track was plainly visible by it, and thus one source of anxiety was removed.

Up to this time Glen had no idea of what had happened, nor of the cause of the shooting that had resulted so disastrously. Now, though he did not turn his head, he learned, from the conversation between the conductor and his fireman, whom the former called "General," that an attempt had been made to rob the train of a large sum of money that the latter had placed in a safe in the express-car. He had received secret information that such an attempt would probably be made, and had engaged two detectives in St. Louis to guard his treasure. When the train was stopped in the woods by a danger signal waved across the track, the engine-driver had been ordered by the would-be robbers, who had cut the express-car loose from those behind it, to go ahead. His refusal to obey them had cost him his life, and the fireman an ugly wound.

The general, who left the sleeper, and ran ahead at the first alarm, had shot and severely injured two of the robbers, and with the aid of his men had driven the rest to the shelter of the forest after a few minutes sharp fighting. The three wounded men, together with the body of the dead engine-driver, were now in the baggage-car; while the train-load of passengers, thanks to the practical knowledge of a sixteen-year-old boy, and the pluck that enabled him to utilize **it,** were rapidly nearing their journey's end in safety.

An anxious crowd was gathered about the Kansas City station as the train rolled slowly up to its platform. The general wrung Glen's hand warmly as he said,

"God bless you, boy, for what you have just done. I will see you again in a few minutes. Now I must look after the wounded men."

Thus saying, he sprang to the platform, leaving Glen in the cab of the locomotive; but when he returned, fifteen minutes later, the boy had disappeared, and was nowhere to be found.

CHAPTER IX.

KANSAS CITY IN EARLY DAYS.

THE reason that Glen Eddy disappeared after running that engine so splendidly, and bringing the night express safely to its destination, was that he was diffident and nervous. Now that the strain was relaxed and he had time to think of the terrible risks run by that train while under his inexperienced guidance, he was seized with a sudden fright. Queerly enough, he felt almost guilty, as though he had done something wrong, or to be ashamed of. Suppose somebody should try to thank him. Suppose the crowd, now surging about the door of the baggage-car, should turn their attention to him, and come to gaze at him as a part of the show that had attracted them. What should he do in either case? It would be unbearable. He must make good his escape before either of these things happened.

The wounded men were being carefully lifted from one side of the baggage-car. Everybody's attention was for the moment directed to that spot. So Glen slipped down from the locomotive cab on the opposite side, and ran back to the sleeper in which were his belongings. The car was deserted and empty. Its passengers, and everybody connected with it, had either gone up town or joined the curious throng about the baggage-car. Thus nobody saw the boy, as, securing his valise and rifle, he slipped from the rear end of the car and walked rapidly away. He plunged into one of the tunnel-like streets running back from the railroad, not knowing, nor caring, where it would lead him. His only idea was to escape, he did not even know from what. It had so taken possession of him, that he almost felt as though he were being pursued, with the danger, at any moment, of being overtaken, and dragged ignominiously back to be—thanked and made a hero of.

Kansas City, which has since enjoyed such an astonishing growth and prosperity, was at that time very young. It was still burrowing through the high and steep bank of stiff red clay that separated its river front from the main street of the newer portion perched on the bluff. Several cross streets, connecting these two parts of the city, had been dug out with infinite labor, to a great depth through the red clay, and it was up one of these that Glen now walked.

He was so far below the level of the airy building-lots on either side that he could not see whether they were occupied or not. Only an occasional long flight of wooden steps, leading up from the street, led him to suppose they might be. He was beginning to wonder where the city was, or if there were any more of it beyond the straggling business street that bordered the railroad, when he came to the main thoroughfare of the new town, and gazed about him with amazement. Although it was yet so early that the sun had only just risen, the broad avenue presented a scene of the most lively activity.

In Brimfield the erection of a new house, or building of any kind, was a matter of general interest that afforded a topic of conversation for weeks. Here were dozens, yes, scores of them, springing up in every direction. A few were of brick; but most of those intended for business purposes were long and low, though furnished with pretentious false fronts that towered as high again as the roof itself. Everywhere was heard the din of hammer and saw, or the ring of the mason's trowel, and in every direction Glen could see the city growing, spreading, and assuming new aspects as he gazed.

At length a pang of hunger recalled him to his present situation, and he inquired of a man, who was hurrying past, the way to the Kaw House.

"Up there a piece," answered the man almost without pausing, and pointing vaguely up the street. "There comes the surveyor's wagon from there now," he added, nodding his head towards one, drawn by two mules, that was dashing in their direction at that moment.

The surveyor's wagon. Then, perhaps, Mr. Brackett was in it, thought Glen. Acting on the impulse of the moment, he sprang into the middle of the street, and waved his rifle in the faces of the advancing mules. The driver reined them in sharply, and the team came to a standstill. "Hello, young fellow, what do you want now?" he shouted.

"I want to know if Mr. Brackett is in this wagon," answered Glen.

"Yes, he is, and that's my name," said a pleasant-faced young man, dressed in a red-flannel shirt, a pair of army trousers tucked into his boot-legs, and what had once been a stylish cutaway coat, who sat beside the driver. "What can I do for you?"

For answer Glen handed him Mr. Hobart's note, which the young man glanced quickly through.

"I see by this that you are to be a member of our party," he said, as he finished reading it, "and that the chief will not be here for a day or two

6

yet. I am very glad to make your acquaintance, Mr. Matherson. Boys, this is Mr. Glen Matherson, our new— Well, we will see what position he will occupy later. Now, Matherson, we are off for our day's work. Would you rather accompany us into the thick of the fray, or will you wend your weary way to the hotel, and while away the hours until our return, surrounded by its gloomy grandeur?"

" I think I would rather go with you, sir," replied Glen, who did not know whether to laugh or not at Mr. Brackett's words and tone.

" 'Tis well, and go with us you shall. So tumble into the chariot, and stow yourself away wherever you can find room. Then let us on with speed."

"But I left Mr. Hobart's things and some of my own on board the train," said Glen, hesitatingly, "and here are the checks for them."

This difficulty was settled by the hailing of a dray, and instructing its driver to get the articles called for by the checks, and carry them, together with Glen's valise, to the hotel. The boy could not bear to trust his precious rifle out of his sight, and so carried it with him.

They had hardly started, when Mr. Brackett turned to Glen and asked him if he had been to breakfast.

This was a question in which the boy was greatly interested just at that moment, and he answered very promptly that he had not.

"Well, here's a go!" exclaimed the other. "A rule of this party is, Matherson, and I hope I shall never be obliged to repeat it to you, that if a man hath not eaten, neither shall he work. It is now too late to return to Delmonico's, so we must intrust you to the tender mercies of the Princess, and may she have mercy upon your appetite. Joe, drive to the palace."

The "palace" proved to be a patchwork shanty of the most unique and surprising description. It was constructed of bits of board, pieces of boxes and barrels, stray shingles and clapboards, roofing-paper, and a variety of other odds and ends. Its doors and windows had evidently been taken from some wrecked steamboat. It was overrun with roses and honeysuckles; while within and without it was scrupulously neat and clean.

As the surveyor's wagon with its noisy load drew up before this queer establishment, its mistress appeared at the door. She was a fat, jolly-looking negress, wearing a gay calico dress, and a still more brilliant turban, and she was immediately greeted with shouts of "How are you, Princess?" "Good-morning, Princess!" "How's her royal nibs to-day?" etc., to all of which she smiled and bowed, and courtesied with the utmost good-nature.

The moment he could make himself heard, Mr. Brackett said, " Princess, we have here a fainting wayfarer. Can you provide him with a cup of nectar ?"

" Yes, sah."

" A dish of peacock's tongues ?"

" Sartin, sah."

" And a brace of nightingale's eggs on toast ?"

" In about free minutes, sah."

" Very well, hasten the feast and speed our departure ; for we must hence, ere many nimble hours be flown."

While waiting for his breakfast to be prepared, Glen had a chance to examine his new companions somewhat more closely than he had yet done. There were eight of them, besides the driver of the wagon, mostly young men, some of them hardly more than boys ; but all strong, healthy looking, and brown from long exposure to sun and wind. Their dress was a medley of flannel, buckskin, and relics of high civilization. They were as merry, careless, and good-natured a set of young fellows as could well be found, always ready for hard work in its time, and equally so for a frolic when the chance offered. They all seemed to be on a perfect equality, called each other by their given names, and played practical jokes upon one another with impunity. As their wagon clattered out of town in the morning, or dashed in again at dusk, its occupants generally sang the most rollicking of college or camp songs, at the top of their voices, and everybody had a kindly word or an indulgent smile for the young surveyors.

Foremost in all their fun was their temporary chief, whom Glen only knew as Mr. Brackett, but who was called "Billy" by all the others. He was about twenty-five years old, and his position was that of transit-man; though, until Mr. Hobart should join the party, he was in charge of it. To Glen, who had thus far only seen him off duty, it was incomprehensible that so frivolous a young man as "Billy" Brackett appeared should hold so responsible a position.

The party had recently returned from the front, where they had been locating a line of new road since earliest spring. Now, while waiting to be sent out again, they were engaged in running in the side tracks, Y's, and switches of what has since become one of the greatest railroad yards in the world. It was on the state line, between Kansas and Missouri, about an hour's drive from the Kaw House, where the surveyors made their headquarters.

In less than five minutes Glen found himself drinking the most delicious cup of coffee he had ever tasted ; while into his hands were thrust a couple of sandwiches of hot corn-pones and crisp bacon. These, with two hard-boiled eggs, furnished a most acceptable meal to the hungry boy. Mr. Brackett tossed a quarter to the "Princess," and the wagon rolled merrily away with Glen eating his breakfast, as best he could, *en route.*

CHAPTER X.

AT WORK WITH THE ENGINEER CORPS.

The "Princess" was a character of those early days, and was celebrated for her *café au lait*, which "Billy" Brackett said meant "coffee and eggs;" but which was really the best of coffee and the richest of goat's milk. Her husband was steward on one of the steamboats that plied up and down the Missouri, and her exertions, added to his, enabled them to accumulate a small property, with which they afterwards made some successful investments in real estate. The boys of the engineer corps were quick to discover the "Princess" after their arrival in the place, and with her they were prime favorites.

Glen had hardly finished his breakfast when the party reached the place where they were to begin work. Here the boy obtained his first knowledge of the names and uses of the various objects that had attracted his curiosity as they lay in the bottom of the wagon.

From their neat wooden boxes were taken

two highly polished brass instruments, each
of which was provided with a telescope. One
of these was a transit, for laying off lines,
angles, and curves on the surface of the earth;
and the other was a level for measuring the
height of elevations or the depth of depressions
on this same surface. As these instruments
were lifted carefully from their boxes they were
screwed firmly to the tops of wooden tripods,
that supported them at the height of a man's
eyes.

Then came the long rod, divided into feet and
the decimal fractions of a foot, that was to be used
with the level, and two slender flag-poles painted
red and white, so as to be seen at long distances.
At their lower ends these poles were tipped with
sharp iron points, and at the other they bore
small flags of red flannel. They went with the
transit, and were to designate the points at
which the sights were to be taken through its
telescope.

There was a one-hundred-foot steel chain,
having links each one foot long, with which to
measure distances. With it went ten slender
steel pins, each eighteen inches long, to the tops
of which bits of red flannel were tied, so that
they could be readily seen. The head chainman carried all of these to start with, and stuck

one into the ground at the end of each hundred feet. The rear chainman gathered them up as he came to them, and thus, by counting the number of pins in his hand, he always knew just what distance had been measured.

The man having charge of or "running" the transit was called the transit-man; the one running the level was called the leveller; while the other members of the party were designated as rodman, front and back flagmen, or "flags," chainmen, and axemen. There were generally two of these last named, and their duty was to clear away timber, brush, or other obstructions on the line, and to make and drive stakes wherever they were needed.

As the several members of the party were preparing for their respective duties, Mr. Brackett put Glen through a sort of an examination, to discover for what particular task he was best fitted.

"I don't suppose, Matherson," he began, "that you care to run the transit to-day?"

"No," laughed Glen, "I think not to-day."

"Nor the level?"

"No, sir.   I'd rather not try it."

"Well, I guess you'd better not.   You might get it out of adjustment.   Can you read a rod?"

No, Glen could not read a rod.

He proved equally ignorant of the duties of flagman, chainman, and axeman, which Mr. Brackett said was very fortunate, as all these positions were already so capably filled in his party that he should really hate to discharge anybody to make room for the new arrival. "But," he added, "I have a most important place left, that I believe you will fill capitally. Can you reproduce the letters of the alphabet and the Arabic numerals on a bit of white pine with a piece of red chalk?"

Somewhat bewildered by this banter, Glen answered rather doubtfully that he believed he could.

"Good! Then you shall stay with the wagon to-day, and mark stakes with this bit of 'kiel'" (red chalk).

So Glen's first day's duty as a civil-engineer was to mark stakes with figures to denote the distance measured, or with various letters, such as P. T. (point of tangent), P. C. (point of curve), etc., for the transit party, and B. M. (bench mark), C. (cut), F. (fill), G. (grade), etc., for the levellers.

Mr. Brackett explained the meaning of these signs patiently and clearly to the boy, whose quick wit enabled him readily to comprehend all that was told him. By noon he was furnishing stakes, properly marked, for the various purposes required, as well as though he had been engaged in this business for a month. It was not a very important position, to be sure; but he filled it to the very best of his ability, which is the most that can be expected of any boy.

One of the things by which the new member was most strongly impressed, during this first day's experience, was the great difference between Mr. Brackett on duty and the same gentleman during his hours of relaxation. While at work he was grave and dignified, nor did he tolerate any familiarity from those who obeyed his orders. And they did obey them promptly, without question or hesitation. He was no longer "Billy;" but was carefully addressed as "Mr. Brackett" by every member of the party. It was evident that he not only thoroughly understood his business, but as thoroughly understood the temper of his men. It was clear, also, that they were well aware that he was not a man to allow his authority to be questioned or trifled with. With this mutual understanding the work progressed smoothly and satisfactorily.

All this was a study in character of which Glen was wise enough to learn the lesson; and perhaps it was the most valuable one of that day's schooling. The discipline of a well-drilled engineer corps is very similar to that maintained on board ship; and, while at certain seasons it may be greatly relaxed, it can, and must, be resumed at a moment's notice, if the authority necessary to produce the best results is to be respected.

The same merry, rollicking party rode back into Kansas City that evening that had left it in the morning; and, though Glen was very tired, he had become well enough acquainted with them to enter heartily into the spirit of the fun. Thus, whenever they sang a song he knew, his voice was heard among the loudest.

At the hotel they learned for the first time of the attempt to rob the train Glen had come on, and wondered that he had said nothing of the affair. When they questioned him, he did not know how to talk of it without proclaiming his share in the night's work, and so only said that, as he was asleep when the fight took place, he had seen nothing of it.

Long after Glen had gone to bed that night, Mr. Brackett, the leveller, and the rodman sat up hard at work on the maps and profiles of the lines they had run that day. If Glen had seen this he would have realized what he afterwards learned, that while the work of most men ends with the day, that of an engineer in the field only ends with bedtime, and sometimes a late one at that.

For two days longer Glen worked with this congenial party, gaining valuable knowledge with each hour, and thoroughly enjoying his new life.

On the third day Mr. Hobart came, and it seemed to Glen like seeing one from home to meet him again. After their first greeting, the engineer said,

"Well, my boy, what other wonderful deeds have you been performing since you and the governor ran the locomotive?"

"The governor!" almost gasped Glen. "Was he a governor?"

"Certainly he was, or rather had been. Didn't you know it? He was General Elting, the ex-governor whom you were inquiring about in St. Louis, and who is now the treasurer of our road. He returned to St. Louis almost immediately from here, and there I heard the whole story from his own lips. He was greatly disappointed at your disappearance, and much pleased to find out that I knew you; for of course I recognized you from his description. He hopes to meet you again some time, and I have promised to see that you do not indulge in any more mysterious disappearances."

While they talked of that night, and its tragic incidents, Mr. Hobart suddenly interrupted himself with,

"By the way, Glen, I am not going to take charge of this locating-party, after all, and so cannot give you a position in it."

Glen felt his face growing pale as he repeated slowly and incredulously,

"Not going to take charge of it?"

"No; I have been relieved of my command, and am going to engage in another kind of work," replied the engineer, smiling at the boy's startled and distressed expression.

Chapter XI.

IF Glen had detected that smile on Mr. Hobart's face, he would have been spared a few moments of very unhappy reflections. He would have known that his brown-bearded friend could not smile while dashing his high hopes, and that there must be something pleasant back of it all. But as the engineer, who could not resist the temptation to try the effects of a disappointment on the boy's temper, turned away his face at that moment, his words were heard, while the smile was not noticed.

Like a great surging wave, the thought of an ignominious return to Brimfield, and a picture of the mill and the store as he had last seen them, swept over the boy's mind. Then came the more recent picture of the happy out-of-door life he had been leading for the past three days. How could he give up the one and go back to the other? Of course, if Mr. Hobart said he could no longer have work with the surveying-party, it must be so. There could be no appeal

from that decision. And he had tried so hard
to do well whatever had been given him to do,
and to make himself useful! It was too bad!
But surely there must be other work in this big,
bustling, wide-awake West, even for a boy. With
this thought his clouded face cleared, and a look
of settled resolve overspread it.

"I'm awfully sorry, sir," he said; but the tone
was almost cheerful, and Mr. Hobart's face was
now the one that expressed surprise. If he had
been able to examine Glen's mind, he would have
seen that the boy had simply decided not to go
back, at least not until the summer was over, but
to stay where he was, and attempt to solve the
bread-and-butter problem alone.

"My new orders came very unexpectedly,"
continued the engineer, "and have completely
upset my plans. It seems that the company has
decided to send me through to the Pacific with
General Lyle's exploring expedition."

A lump rose in Glen's throat. General Lyle's
expedition! Why, that was the one Binney
Gibbs was to accompany. Was all the world
going on that wonderful trip except himself? It
almost seemed so. "It will be a fine trip, sir,"
he said, trying to choke down the lump.

"Yes, I suppose it will; but it will also be a
hard and dangerous one, such as a great many

people would not care to undertake. I don't
suppose you would, for instance?" and Mr. Hobart looked quizzically at the boy.

"Wouldn't I! I'd just like to have somebody
offer me a chance to go on that expedition, that's
all!"

"Very well," replied the engineer, quietly, "I'll
offer you the chance, just to see whether you will
accept it or not. Will you go with me on this
long trip?"

For a few seconds Glen gazed into the brown-
bearded face without answering. Was he awake
or dreaming? Had the words been spoken? Do
you really mean it, sir?" he almost gasped, at
length, "or are you only making fun of me!"

"Mean it? of course I do," was the reply. I
generally mean what I say, and if you really
care to explore Kansas and Colorado, New Mexico, Arizona, and Southern California in my company, I shall be most happy to have you do so.
I am also authorized to offer you a position, a
humble one, to be sure, but one that will pay the
same salary that you would have received as a
member of the locating-party, in the division I
am to command. I don't suppose there will be
many chances for you to run locomotives out
there; but I have no doubt there will be plenty
of swimming to be done, as well as other things

7

in the line of your peculiar abilities. But you have not answered my question yet. Will you accept my offer, or do you wish a few days in which to consider it?"

"Oh, Mr. Hobart!" cried the boy, who was standing up in his excitement. "It seems almost too good to be true! I can't realize that this splendid chance, that I've been trying so hard not to think about, has really come to me. Why, I'd rather go on that trip than do anything else in the whole world, and if you'll only take me along, in any position, I don't care what, I'll be grateful to you all my life."

"But what do you think your father will say? Do you suppose he will let you go?" inquired the engineer, soberly.

Glen's face became grave again in an instant. "Oh, yes, he's sure to," he replied, "but I'll write this very minute, and ask him.

"There won't be time to receive an answer," said Mr. Hobart, "for we must start from here to-morrow; but perhaps this letter will make things all right. You see," he added, "I thought it was just possible that you might care to accept my offer, and so I took the liberty of writing and asking your father if he were willing to have you do so. I also asked him not to say anything about it in Brimfield until after we had started, for fear I should be flooded with applications from other boys, who might imagine I had the power to give them positions. Your father's answer reached me here an hour ago, and with it came this letter for you."

No own father could have written a kinder or more satisfactory letter to a boy than the one Mr. Matherson sent to his adopted son. It readily granted the required permission, and congratulated Glen upon the splendid opportunity thus opened to him. At the same time it told him how they already missed him, and how they hated the thought of not seeing him for a whole year. It closed with the information that Binney Gibbs was making extensive preparations for his departure to the far West, and that the famous expedition, of which he was to be a member, was the all-absorbing topic of conversation in Brimfield.

Mr. Hobart watched the boy's glowing face as he read this letter with genuine pleasure; for he had taken a real liking to him, and was not only glad of this opportunity for affording him such unalloyed happiness, but also that they were to be companions on the proposed trip.

Matters being thus happily settled, the engineer told Glen that they would start the following evening for the end of the track, nearly two hundred miles west of that point, where the expedition was to rendezvous, and where he was to establish a camp for their reception.

The information that interested and pleased Glen the most, though, was that Mr. Brackett was to be assistant engineer of the new division, and that most of the members of the party with whom the boy was already on such friendly terms, were also to join it.

Being dismissed by Mr. Hobart, with orders to be on hand bright and early in the morning, for the morrow would be a busy day, the happy lad rushed away to find those who were to be his fellow-explorers, and talk over with them the wonders and delights of the proposed trip. To his surprise not one of them was anywhere about the hotel, and he was told that the entire party had gone down town a few moments before. Too excited to do anything else, Glen immediately set out to find them. For some time he searched in vain; but at length, attracted by the sound of great shouting and laughter, he joined a throng of people who were gathered about one of the few barber shops of the city, and seemed to be vastly entertained by something taking place inside.

Recognizing "Billy" Brackett's voice above all the other sounds that came from the shop,

Glen pushed himself forward until he finally gained a position inside the door. All the engineers were there. Three of them occupied the three chairs that the shop boasted, and were having their hair cut. Another, standing on a table, so that he could overlook the crowd, was superintending the operation. But for his voice and his unmistakable costume, Glen would never have recognized in him the dignified young engineer under whom he had been at work but an hour before. Every spear of hair had disappeared from his head, and he was as bald as a billiard cue. Seated on the table, contentedly swinging their legs, were two other bald-headed figures, whom Glen with difficulty recognized as the leveller and rodman.

When the three victims in the chairs had been reduced to a similar state of baldness, their places were instantly occupied by the remaining members of the party. The whole performance was conducted amid the most uproarious fun, of which the recently promoted assistant engineer was the ruling spirit.

As the chairs became empty for the third time, and the nine bald-headed members prepared to depart, each declaring that the others were the most comical-looking objects he had ever seen, they suddenly caught sight of Glen, and a rush was made for him.   In another moment, despite his struggles, he too was seated in a barber's chair, and was rapidly growing as bald as his fellow-explorers.

"You'll look worse than a boiled owl, Glen," remarked "Billy" Brackett, encouragingly.

"And be a living terror to Injuns," cried another.

"It'll be the greatest comfort in the world, old man, to feel that though you may be killed, you can't be scalped," shouted a third.

Realizing that resistance was useless, Glen submitted to the shearing process with as good a grace as possible.   A few minutes later, wearing a very loose-fitting hat, he was marching up the street with his jovial comrades, joining with the full strength of his lungs in the popular chorus of

"The bald-headed man, who's been always in the van
  Of everything that's going, since the world first began."

Chapter XII.

Transforming themselves into a party of bald-heads was the last of the absurd pranks with which the young engineers entertained the good people of Kansas City for many a long day. At the same hour on the following evening they were well on their way towards the far West in a dilapidated passenger-coach attached to a freight train loaded with tents and supplies of every description for their long trip.

By the next noon, after a hard, rough ride of nearly two hundred miles, the end of the track was reached. It was on a treeless prairie, sweeping away as far as the eye could see on all sides. Here was spread a thick green carpet of short buffalo grass, and into this carpet were woven exquisite patterns of innumerable flowers. The place was at the junction of the Kaw River with one of its numerous branches, and where but a few weeks before wild Indians had camped and vast herds of buffalo had pastured, a railroad town of several hundred rough frame houses,

shanties, and tents had already sprung into ex·
istence.

Here the overland stages took their departure
for the distant mining town of Denver, and here
the long trains of great freight-wagons were loaded for their toilsome journey over the Sante Fé
trail to the far-away valley of the Rio Grande.
Here, on side-tracks, were the construction-cars,
movable houses on wheels, in which lived the
graders, track-layers, and other members of the
army of workmen employed in the building of a
railroad.   Railroad men, soldiers, teamsters, trad-
ers, Indians, and Mexicans, horses, mules, and oxen
mingled here in picturesque confusion.   Nearly
every man carried a rifle, and it was rare to meet
one who did not wear one or more revolvers
strapped to his waist.

It was by far the most novel and bustling scene
Glen had ever looked upon ; and, as he stepped
from the last railroad-car he was to see for many
months, and stretched his cramped limbs, he gazed
about him in astonishment. But there was no time
for idling, and Glen had hardly given a glance at
his unfamiliar surroundings before Mr. Hobart's
voice, saying, " Come, boys, there's plenty to do,
and but a few hours to do it in," set the whole
party to work in the liveliest possible manner.

There was a fine grassy level about a hundred

yards from the railroad, on the opposite side from the settlement. It was skirted by a clear but sluggish stream, fringed by a slender growth of cottonwood-trees, and was so evidently the very place for a camp that Mr. Hobart selected it at once. Here the young engineers worked like beavers all through that long, hot afternoon, and by nightfall they had pitched twenty wall-tents, arranged in the form of an open square. One of these was reserved for Mr. Hobart, while Mr. Brackett and the leveller were given another, and two more were allowed to the other members of the party. Into these they had removed all their personal belongings, while in two other tents, carefully ditched and banked to keep out the water in case of rain, were stored all the instruments, implements, blank-books, and stationery provided for the expedition.

Heartily tired after this novel but interesting labor, how Glen did enjoy his tin-cup of black coffee without milk, the fried bacon and hard-tack, that constituted his supper, when, at sundown, one of the axemen, who had been at work for an hour over a fire, announced that it was ready! He would have scorned such fare at home; but, with his present appetite, and under the circumstances, it seemed as though nothing had ever tasted better.

As the darkness came on, how cheerful the tent, that had now become his home, looked in the light of a lantern hung from its ridge-pole! What a pleasant hour he passed listening to the stories and experiences of his three tentmates, as they lay luxuriously outstretched on their blankets, enjoying their well-earned rest! The entire stock of blankets was used to make one wide, comfortable bed for the four. All the rubbers were, of course, placed underneath, next the ground, and Glen was greatly pleased at the praise bestowed upon his rubber-sheet, which was twice as large as an ordinary blanket, and which he had followed Mr. Hobart's advice in procuring.

After the others had finished their evening pipes and dropped off to sleep, and after the light had been put out, the novelty of this first night under canvas kept Glen awake for some time. What a fortunate fellow he felt himself to be, as he lay there recalling the events of the last ten days, and trying to picture the immediate future! To think that he, the worst scholar in his class, a boy without an own father or mother, so far as he knew, nor even a birthday that he was sure of, should be away out here on the Plains, and about to start on an expedition that every boy in the country would be thankful to join if he could. It was simply wonderful; and he resolved that, if hard work and the promptest possible attention to duty could render him worthy of such good-fortune, neither of these things should be lacking.

By daylight the camp was astir; but Glen was the first to roll out of his blankets, and he had been down to the creek for a plunge in its cool waters before breakfast-time. Then followed another hard day's work. The train of twenty heavy canvas-topped army-wagons, each drawn by six mules, the three four-mule ambulances, and the drove of spare animals furnished to the expedition by the government, arrived during the morning. These wagons had to be loaded with the vast quantity of provisions and various supplies brought thus far by rail. Then the tents already up had to be ditched, and still others erected for the use of the engineer-in-chief and other officers of the party who were now hourly expected to arrive.

A flag-pole was planted in front of the head-quarter tents, and that evening, when a train came in bringing General Lyle and about half the members of the expedition, an American flag was run to its top. Both it and the general were greeted with a volley of rifle-shots and a hearty cheer, while at the same time the encampment was christened "Camp Lyle."

Glen's youthful appearance attracted the chief's attention as soon as he caught sight of the lad, and he was inclined to doubt the advisability of allowing such a mere boy to accompany the expedition. A few words from Mr. Hobart satisfied him, however, that Glen would prove a credit to the party, and after that the general watched the boy with interest.

With the chief-engineer came a geologist, botanist, surgeon, photographer, private secretary, quartermaster, the two other division commanders, and, what was of more immediate interest to all the young engineers, several good camp-cooks. Thus, on the second night of its existence, with this large increase in the number of its occupants, Camp Lyle presented a most cheerful and animated appearance.

Early the following morning another train arrived from the East, bringing the remaining members of the expedition. A few minutes after its arrival Glen was awakened by hearing a voice that sounded very familiar, calling,

"Hello! I say! Some of you fellows come out here and help me'!'

As he sat up in his blankets, wondering who could be speaking with such a tone of authority, and whether he ought to answer the summons or not, a head was thrust into the tent-door, and the demand was repeated.

It was Binney Gibbs, who had passed as completely out of Glen's mind as though he had never existed. He did not recognize Glen's bald head; but, when the latter stepped from the tent with his hat on, saying, " Hello, Binney, old man, what can I do for you ?" the prize scholar of the Brimfield High School stood for a moment speechless with amazement.

"You here ?" he finally stammered. " What on earth does it mean ?"

" It means," replied Glen, laughing at the other's incredulous expression, " that Brimfield is to have two representatives on this expedition instead of one, and that I am going through to the Pacific with you."

Binney had always been jealous of Glen, but at that moment he felt that he almost hated him.

In spite of this, he allowed his former schoolmate and another stout fellow to bring his heavy trunk from the railroad into camp. When the quartermaster saw it he said that, as there would be no room for trunks in the wagons, the owner of this one must take from it what would fill a moderate-sized valise, and either dispose of the trunk with the rest of its contents or send them back home. To this Binney angrily replied that he would see General Lyle about it.

The new arrival gave further offence that morning by turning up his nose at the breakfast prepared by one of the camp-cooks, and declaring it unfit for white men to eat. He also refused, point-blank, to help unload a car when requested to do so by one of the division engineers, saying that it was not the kind of work he had been engaged to perform.

He was only brought to a realizing sense of his position by a severe reprimand from General Lyle himself, who declared that, upon the next complaint brought to him of the boy's conduct, he should discharge him. He also said that only the fact of Binney's having been sent there by his old friend Mr. Meadows prevented him from doing so at once. The chief closed his remarks by advising Binney to take the other Brimfield boy of the party as an example worthy of copying. Thereupon all the prize scholar's bitterness of feeling was directed against unsuspecting Glen, and he vowed he would get even with that young nobody yet.

Chapter XIII.

BINNEY GIBBS AND HIS MULE.

The effect on Binney Gibbs of General Lyle's reprimand was good, inasmuch as it brought him to a realizing sense of his true position in that party, and showed him that, if he wished to remain a member of it, he must obey orders, even when they were issued in the form of polite requests. So, after that, he made a virtue of necessity, and obeyed every order with a scrupulous exactness, though generally with an injured air, and a protesting expression of countenance as though he were being imposed upon. It was a great mortification to him to be obliged to send home his trunk, and more than half his supply of clothing, together with a number of other cherished luxuries, such as a rubber bathtub, a cork mattress, a rubber pillow, half a dozen linen sheets, several china plates, cups, and saucers, besides some silver and plated ware, all of which he relinquished with a heavy heart and many lamentations.

The only thing in the shape of a valise, with

which to replace his trunk, that he could purchase in the railroad settlement, was one of those cheap affairs made of glazed leather, such as are often seen in the hands of newly landed immigrants. As Binney brought this into the camp, it at once attracted universal attention. The boys crowded about him, begging to be allowed to examine his new and elegant " grip-sack ;" and, from that day forth, he was known as "Grip" by the entire party.

For a week longer the expedition remained at Camp Lyle, waiting for settled weather, and preparing for its great undertaking. It was divided into four divisions, three of which were regularly equipped surveying-parties who were to run transit and level lines from a point near the Colorado border to the Pacific Ocean. The fourth, or headquarter division, was composed of the commander and his immediate staff, together with the scientific men and their assistants.

As Glen hoped and expected, he was assigned to the second division, of which Mr. Hobart was engineer in charge, and Mr. Brackett was assistant. He was a little disappointed that the only position found for him in the division was the very lowest of all in rank and pay. It was that of tapeman, and his duties were to assist the topographer of the party in measuring distances to, or taking the bearings of, prominent objects along the line. Neither could Glen help wishing that Binney Gibbs had not been assigned to the same division as himself. On account of his brilliant record for scholarship and skill with figures, Binney was made rodman, a position that far outranked Glen's and commanded twice his pay. Still, Glen strove hard not to feel envious of this other Brimfield boy. He was altogether too proud of being a member of the expedition on any terms to have room for any other feeling, and he was anxious to be on a friendly footing with Binney, as he was with everybody else. So, when the positions were announced, and the prize scholar was found to hold such a fine one, Glen was the first to tender his congratulations.

Binney received them coldly, merely remarking that they could not very well have given him any lower position, and that he should not have accepted anything less if it had been offered.

Glen only smiled at this, and thought how fortunate it was that he did not feel that way.

As a rodman Binney was allowed the use of a saddle-animal, and a very small mule was assigned to him as his mount. When he went down to the wagons to inspect his new acquisition, he

8

thought he had never seen a more dangerous-looking animal. It laid back its ears and bit at him when he attempted to pat it on the nose, and manifested every other sign of mulish antipathy towards its new master. In spite of all this, the teamster having it in charge assured Binney that it was a perfect lamb, and the rodman, anxious to prove his ability to ride a mule, which some of the boys had doubted, ordered the animal to be saddled.

The man who held the beast while Binney climbed awkwardly into the saddle winked at some of his fellows who were watching the operation, and thrust his tongue derisively into his cheek.

For a few moments the mule did prove a veritable lamb, ambling along so gently that Binney's spirits rose, and he began to imagine himself the rider that he claimed to be. Elated by his success, he even dared to give the bridle reins a shake, say "Get up!" and finally to touch the side of his steed with the spur that, in his pride, he had fastened to one of his boot-heels.

The effect was electrical. In an instant Binney found himself hatless, with both feet out of the stirrups, clinging for dear life to the pommel of the saddle, and wishing himself anywhere but on the back of a mule dashing madly, at full speed, directly into camp.

"Help! help!" he shouted, breathlessly. "Head him off! stop him somebody!"

Once inside that square of tents, the mule did not seem to realize the possibility of again passing beyond them, but tore frantically round and round the inner side of the square, as though it were a circus-ring. Everybody dropped his work and rushed out to witness the comical spectacle.

"Freeze to him, Grip!" cried one.

"Give him his head!"

"What made you leave Barnum's?"

"Stand up on his back!"

"Don't abuse the poor mule! It's a shame to make him run so!"

These, and a hundred similar cries, mingled with shouts of uproarious laughter, greeted poor Binney from all sides; while not the slightest attention was paid to his piteous entreaties that somebody would stop the mule.

At length these cries seemed to attract the attention of the animal himself; for he suddenly planted his fore-feet and stopped so abruptly that Binney was flung over his head as from a catapult. Then the mule lifted high his head and uttered a prolonged ear-splitting bray of defiance.

Glen had sprung forward and caught the animal's bridle almost the instant he stopped. Now leading him to where Binney sat, dazed but unhurt, he asked, soberly, "Do you want to try him again, Binney?"

"Try him again!" shouted the rodman, angrily. "No, I never want to see him again; but if you think he's easy to ride, why don't you try him yourself?"

"Yes, try him, young 'un! Give him another turn around the ring, Glen!" shouted the spectators, anxious to have their fun prolonged, but having no idea that this boy from Brimfield could ride, any more than the other.

Glen borrowed a pair of spurs, soothed the mule for a moment, sinched the girth a trifle tighter, and, with a sudden leap, vaulted into the saddle. For an instant the animal remained motionless with astonishment; then he bounded into the air, and came down with all four legs as stiff as posts. The shock would have been terrible to the boy, had he not lifted himself from the saddle and supported his whole weight in the stirrups. The mule repeated this movement several times, and then began to plunge and kick. But the saddle in which Glen sat was a deeply hollowed, high-pommelled, Mexican affair, built for just such occasions as this, and so the plunging might have been kept up all day without disturbing the rider in the least.

The mule laid down and tried to roll, while the boy, who had jumped from his back, stood quietly by, and allowed him to discover the folly of the attempt. The high pommel of the sad dle again interfered; and as the disgusted animal scrambled to his feet, he again found his burr-like rider as firmly seated on his back as ever.

For a moment the mule hung his head in a dejected manner, as though thinking out some new plan. Suddenly his meditations were interrupted by a yell directly in one of his long ears, and a sharp pain felt in both sides at once. He sprang forward to escape these annoyances; but they clung to him as close as did his new rider. Faster and faster he flew, while harder and harder spurred Glen, and louder grew his yells. All at once the animal stopped, as short as on the former occasion; but this time the rider did not fly over his head. The fact is, the mule was now so thoroughly frightened and bewildered that he had no idea of stopping until his lower jaw was jerked back so sharply that had it belonged to any other kind of an animal it must have been dislocated. Even Glen had no idea of the power of that cruel Mexican bit, and was almost as greatly surprised as the mule at its sudden effect.

Then came more yelling, more spurring, and more frantic dashing around that tiresome square. At length the mule spied the opening through which he had entered, and, rushing through it, he sped away over the open prairie, thankful to be rid of those bewildering tents and shouting spectators, even though his rider still clung as close as ever to that Mexican saddle.

When the two returned to camp, half an hour later, it was evident that the most perfect understanding existed between them; but the mule was so crestfallen by his humiliation that for a long time even Binney Gibbs could ride and abuse him with impunity.

As for Glen, his reputation as a horseman was firmly established, and from that day until he got a horse of his own there was always somebody willing and anxious to place a mount at his disposal.

Chapter XIV.

A FEW mornings after Glen's experience with the mule, the white tents of Camp Lyle were struck; and at sunrise the long slow-moving trains of wagons had covered the first mile of the many hundreds lying between it and the Pacific. The last railroad had been left behind, and the sound of its whistle was heard no more. Already our young explorer was learning, from his more experienced comrades, to distinguish an Indian pony and lodge-pole trail from that of a buffalo, and a buffalo wallow from an ordinary mud-hole. Already he had seen his first prairie-dog town, and had gazed curiously at several bleached skulls of the mighty bison, some of which were still partially covered with shaggy hair. Already, too, he was filled with that sense of glorious freedom and boundless possibility that can on.y be breathed with the air of unlimited space. Glen was surprised to find that, instead of being level, as he had always thought them, the Plains rolled, in vast undulations, having a general north and south direction, so that, as the wagons were moving west, they were always ascending some long slope, or descending its farther side. He was almost startled, too, by the intense silence brooding over them, and unbroken at a short distance from the train, save by the plaintive song of meadow-larks.

But nobody was allowed to stray far from the wagons, even to note the silence of the Plains, for fear lest it might be broken by very unpleasant sounds. All the "horse Indians" of the country were leagued together, that summer, to fight the whites. North of the Platte, Sioux, Blackfeet, and Crows had smoked the peace-pipe, and united to harass the builders of the Union Pacific. South of that river, Cheyennes, Kiowas, Comanches, and Arrapahoes were waging common war against those who were turning the buffalo pastures into farms, and making such alarming inroads into the vast herds upon which they depended for meat. The Indians were well armed, well mounted, and determined. Custer, with the Seventh Cavalry, was ranging the Platte valley, and the country between it and the Republican, so that, in that vicinity, Indians were becoming scarce. South of that, however, and particularly along the Smoky Hill, the valley of which General Lyle's expedi-

tion was ascending, Indians had never been more
plentiful or troublesome than now.

Every day brought its rumors of murdered
settlers, captured wagon-trains, besieged stage
stations, and of the heavily guarded stages themselves turned back, or only reaching their destina-
tions after fierce running fights, riddled with bullets, and bearing sad loads of dead and wounded
passengers. Along the entire Smoky Hill route,
from the end of the railroad to Denver, a distance of four hundred miles, were only three
small forts, with garrisons of three or four com-
panies each ; and the strength of these garrisons
was constantly weakened by the demand for es-
corts to stages and emigrant trains. Thus the
exploring expedition was forced to depend largely on its own resources, and must fight its way
through as best it could. Arms were therefore
supplied to all its members who did not possess
them, and, from the outset, a strong camp guard
was posted each night.

At the end of a day's march the wagon-master,
or " wagon-boss," who always rode ahead of the
train mounted on a sleek saddle mule, would
select a camping-ground, generally where wood,
water, and grass were to be had, and, turning
from the beaten trail, would lead the way to it.
Where he halted the first wagon also stopped.

Then he would move on a short distance, and the second wagon would follow him, until it was ordered to wheel into line with the first. When all thus occupied their designated positions, they either formed a semicircle on the bank of the stream, with their poles pointing inward, were arranged in two parallel lines facing each other, or, if the place was very much exposed, they would form a complete circle, with each tongue overlapping the hind-wheels of the wagon before it.

The minute the train halted, all the stock was unharnessed or unsaddled, and, under guard of two mounted teamsters, were allowed to graze on the sweet buffalo grass, within sight of camp, until sunset, when they were watered and driven in. Then each team was fastened to its own wagon and given its ration of corn. All the saddle animals and spare stock were securely picketed within the line of wagons, thus leaving the smallest possible chance for an Indian to get anywhere near them.

While the animals were being thus attended to, the men were hard at work pitching tents, getting out blankets and such baggage as might be needed, collecting fuel for the camp-fires, fetching water for the cooks, and, if the location of the camp was considered especially dangerous, in digging rifle-pits in which the guards for the night would be posted. All this work was performed by regular details, changed each day, and announced each morning at breakfast-time. Thus, one day Glen would find himself on the detail for pitching headquarter tents, and the next answering the cook's imperative demands for water. Or, provided with a gunny-sack, he might be scouring the immediate neighborhood for a supply of dry buffalo chips, with which to eke out the scanty stock of fire-wood. He always performed these tasks cheerfully and faithfully; not that he liked them, but because he realized their necessity, and saw that all the others, below the rank of assistant engineer, were obliged to do the same things.

Binney Gibbs, however, considered such duties irksome and demeaning. He thought it very hard that the son of a wealthy man, a prize scholar, and a rodman, such as he was, should be compelled to act as a cook's assistant. To show his contempt for the work he performed it awkwardly and with much grumbling. The cooks were not slow to discover this; and, as a cook is a power in camp as well as elsewhere, they began to make things as unpleasant as possible for him. It was wonderful how much more water was needed when it was his turn to keep them supplied than it was when any one else was on duty. Then, too, while Glen's willingness and good - nature were rewarded by many a tidbit, slyly slipped into his tin plate, it chanced that Binney always got the toughest pieces of meat, the odds and ends of everything, and, whenever he asked for a second helping, was told that there was none of that particular dish left. He tried to retaliate by complaining of the cooks at headquarters; but, as he could prove nothing against them, the only result of this unwise measure was that he got less to eat than ever, and but for a hard-tack barrel that was always open to everybody would have been on a fair way to starvation.

Another thing Binney hated to do was to stand guard. This duty came to each one in turn, every three or four nights, according to the number of sentinels required, and on a night of duty each one was obliged to keep watch "two hours on and four off." That is, if Binney or Glen went on duty at six o'clock, he would be relieved at eight, and allowed to sleep until midnight, when he would stand guard again at one of the several posts beyond the camp limits, until two. Then he might sleep until six, when, if camp was not already broken, he must again go on duty until it was, and the wagon-train was in motion.

Binney declared this was all nonsense. It was well enough, he said, to talk about Indians attacking a small party, or a stage station here and there; but as for bothering a large, well-armed party like this, they simply wouldn't think of doing such a thing. There was as much danger of their attacking Fort Riley! The idea of waking a fellow up at midnight, and sending him out on the prairie to listen to coyotes and screech-owls for two hours! It was ridiculous! He might as well be enlisted in the army and have done with it! So he growled and grumbled, and tried, in every way possible, to shirk this guard duty, though generally without success.

Even Glen wondered if it were necessary to keep so many men on guard, and if the disagreeable duty did not come oftener than it need. At length, however, something happened to convince these boys that no guard against the wily foes surrounding them could be too strong or too carefully kept.

They had been out a week, and were in the heart of the Indian country, far beyond the most advanced settlements, when, one evening, camp was pitched on a level bit of valley, bounded on one side by bluffs that separated it from the higher plains. On the other side flowed a creek bordered by a growth of cottonwoods, red willows, and tall, rank grass. Beyond the creek rose still other bluffs, forming the eastern boundary of this pleasant valley. From time immemorial the place had been a favorite resort of Indians, as was shown by the abandoned wick-i-ups, lodge-poles, and quantities of bleached buffalo bones found in a grove of great cottonwoods a short distance up the stream. There was, however, nothing to indicate that they had occupied the place recently, and so, though the one topic of conversation about the camp-fires at supper-time was Indians, it was rather of those belonging to other times and places than to the present.

Suddenly, from the top of the bluff behind the camp, came half a dozen shots, and the sentinel who had been posted there rushed in, shouting, "Indians! Indians!" This time the enemy proved to be two overland stages, loaded with mails and troops, who had fought their way through from Denver. These had mistaken the sentinel for an Indian, and fired at him, while he, thinking from this that they certainly must be Indians, had fired back.

Late that same night the camp was again alarmed by a shot from one of its sentries. Everybody sprang from his tent, rifle in hand, and for a few minutes the excitement was in-tense. It was succeeded by a feeling of deep disgust when it was discovered that sentry Binney Gibbs had fired at a coyote that the light of the newly risen moon had disclosed prowling about the camp.

When, therefore, at two o'clock in the morning, Glen went on duty, and was stationed on the edge of the slope leading down to the stream, Mr. Brackett, who was officer of the guard, charged him not to fire at anything unless he was absolutely sure it was an Indian.

Glen answered that he certainly would not give an alarm without good cause for so doing; and Mr. Brackett, promising to visit him again at the end of an hour, went softly away to inspect the next post on his round.

When, at the end of an hour, the officer of the guard returned to the post where he had left Glen, the boy was not to be found. In vain did Mr. Brackett call his name, at first in low tones, and then louder. In vain did he question the other sentries. They had neither seen nor heard anything more suspicious than an occasional coyote. In vain was the whole camp aroused and a search made through its tents and wagons. Not a trace of the boy, who was so universally liked, was to be found. He had disappeared as absolutely, so far as they were concerned, as though the earth had opened and swallowed him.

Chapter XV.

THE SUSPICIOUS MOVEMENTS OF CERTAIN COYOTES.

WHEN Glen was left lying on the ground, with his rifle beside him, peering into the black shadows of the undergrowth, he certainly did not anticipate seeing any thing more dangerous to his own safety, or that of the sleeping camp, than coyotes, and he had already learned what cowardly beasts they were. How absurd it was of Binney Gibbs to fire at one. He might have known what it was. No wonder the fellows were provoked. He would like to know as much as Binney did about some things; but he should hate to be as silly as he in others. How many coyotes there were to-night anyhow. He had already heard their short, sharp barks, and long dismal howls from the bluffs behind him, and from those on the opposite side of the stream. Now another of the weird sounds came floating down on the damp night air from the direction of the old Indian camping-ground. Perhaps that fellow was howling because he couldn't find any meat on those bleached buffalo bones. Well, no wonder. Glen thought he would be inclined to howl, too, over such a disappointment as that.

It was not absolutely dark; for, though the moon was in its last quarter, it gave considerable light when the clouds would let it; but they were scurrying across the sky at such a rate that they kept it hidden most of the time. As Glen was facing the east, it lighted the spot where he lay whenever it was allowed to light any thing, and made the darkness of the underbrush, at which he gazed, blacker than ever. It was forlorn and lonely enough without the moonlight; but Glen thought that perhaps it was better to be in darkness than to be lighted up while enemies might possibly be gazing at him from the safe cover of those impenetrable shadows. How easily a rifle-shot from those bushes could pick him off during one of those uncomfortable little spells of moonlight.

All at once Glen saw another light, apparently on the edge of the opposite bluffs. It showed yellow and steady for a second, and then disappeared. Was it an Indian signal, or a newly risen star suddenly obscured by clouds? This was a question calculated to keep even a sleepy boy wide awake. Perhaps if he watched closely he would see it again. He had heard a great deal about Indian signals lately, and knew that, by flashes of fire at night, smokes, waving blankets, and mirror flashes by day, they could transmit intelligence across the plains almost as readily as white men could do the same thing by telegraph. How he wished he understood their signals, and how he would like to see them using them.

Glen was very curious concerning Indians— real wild ones—and hoped he should at least catch a glimpse of some before the trip was ended. It would be too absurd to return to Brimfield, after crossing the Plains, and to be obliged to confess that he had not met any.

Hallo! How near those coyote howls were coming. Wasn't that one of the brutes now, skulking in the shadow of those willows? Certainly something was moving down there. Now there were two of them. With what an ugly snarl they greeted each other. Still, that snarl was a comfort; for it proved them to be really coyotes. At least so thought Glen. Just then the boy sneezed. He couldn't have helped it to save him, and at the same moment the moon shone out. The coyotes had disappeared. Perhaps they thought he would fire at them, as Binney Gibbs had. But they needn't be afraid. He wasn't going to alarm the camp on account of coyotes.

Another cloud swallowed the moon, and again Glen thought he could distinguish a black object moving through the shadows. Although he strained his eyes, and watched intently, almost holding his breath in his excitement, he could see only one object, and it certainly was moving towards him. Where was the other ? If he only dared fire at that one ! The boy clutched his rifle nervously. The coyote came sneaking on, very slowly, frequently stopping and remaining motionless for several seconds ; but Glen never took his eyes from it. If he only had, just long enough to give one look at the human figure creeping noiselessly towards him from behind ; but no thought of danger from that direction entered his head.

As the Indian, gliding up behind the young sentry, reached a point from which he could distinguish the outlines of the recumbent figure before him, he cautiously raised himself on one knee, and fitted a steel-headed arrow to the bow that had been slung on his back. In another instant it would have sped on its fatal mission, and Glen's career would have ended as suddenly as the snuffing of a candle-flame. He was saved by a gleam of moonlight, that caused the Indian to sink, like a shadow, into the grass. The coyote also remained motionless. Then the moon was again obscured, and the Indian again rose to a crouching posture. He had evidently changed his plans; for he no longer held the bow in his hand. That gleam of moonlight had showed him that the sentry was only a boy, instead of the man he had supposed, and he determined to try for a captive instead of a scalp.

The next instant he sprang forward with the noiseless bound of a panther, and the breath was driven from Glen's body as the Indian lighted on his back, with one hand over the boy's mouth. The coyote rose on its hind-legs, and leaped forward at the same moment. In a twinkling its skin was flung over Glen's head, and so tightly fastened about his neck that he was at once smothered and strangled. He tried to cry out, but could not. He did not even know what had happened, or who these were that, swiftly and with resistless force, were half dragging, half carrying him between them.

For a moment he entertained the wild hope that it was a practical joke of some of the boys from camp. That hope was speedily dispelled; for, as his captors gained the shelter of the trees on the bank of the stream, they halted long enough to secure his arms firmly behind him, and to loosen the coyote-skin so that he could breathe a trifle more freely. Then he was again hurried forward.

After travelling what seemed to the poor boy like an interminable distance, and when he was so faint and dizzy with the heat and suffocation of that horrible wolf-skin that he felt he could not go a step farther, it was suddenly snatched from his head, and the strong grasp of his arms was let go. The boy staggered against the trunk of a tree, and would have fallen but for its support. For a few moments he saw nothing, and was conscious of nothing save the delicious coolness of the air and the delight of breathing it freely once more.

The halt was a short one; for already a faint light, different from that of the moon, was stealing over the eastern bluffs, and the Indians must have their prisoner far away from there by sunrise. There were three of them now, as well as some ponies and a mule. Glen could also see a great many white objects scattered about the ground. They were bleached buffalo bones. As he recognized them, he knew he was at the old Indian camping-ground he had visited the evening before, and from which one of those coyote howls had seemed to come. So it had; but it had been uttered by the young Cheyenne left there in charge of the animals, in answer to the howls of the two other human coyotes, who, prowling about the engineers' camp, had finally made Glen a prisoner.

They were Cheyenne scouts, belonging to the Dog Soldier band, at that time the most famous fighters of that warlike tribe. They had been sent out from their village, on the American Fork, two days before, to find out what they could concerning General Lyle's exploring expedition, rumors of which had already reached the ears of their chiefs. So successfully had they accomplished their mission that they had not only discovered all they wanted to know about these new invaders of their territory, but had actually taken one of their number prisoner. Besides this they had stolen three fine saddle ponies, and a powerful white mule, from the corral of a stage station some twenty miles up the trail. Now, therefore, as they swung their captive on the back of the mule, and secured him by passing a thong of rawhide about his ankles and beneath the animal's belly, their hearts were filled with rejoicing over their success.

Chapter XVI.

ESPECIALLY happy was the youngest of the three Indians, who was a boy of about Glen's age. This was the first scout he had ever been allowed to go on; and, as he reflected upon the glory of their return to the village, with that prisoner, those stolen ponies, and all the valuable information they had acquired, he wondered if there was any happier or prouder boy living than he. He even had a kindly feeling towards the white boy, who, by allowing himself to be captured, had contributed so largely to the honors that would be showered upon him, and he grinned good-humoredly in Glen's face as soon as the growing daylight enabled him to see it plainly. Up to this time the Cheyenne boy had only been known as "Blackbird;" but he had set forth on this scout with the firm determination of winning a name more worthy of a young warrior. Had he not already done so? His companions had complimented him on his carefully executed imitation of a coyote's howl, and one of them had suggested that he must have a veritable wolf's tongue in his mouth: "Wolf-Tongue!" There was a fine name for a young Dog soldier. What if he should be allowed to keep it for his own? There was not another boy of his age in the village with such a name as that. Now he began to make some curious motions with his hands, and poor Glen, who, in spite of his own wretchedness, could not keep from watching him with some curiosity, wondered what the young Indian was up to. Dropping the bridle on his pony's neck, the boy lifted both hands to the level of his shoulders with the first two fingers of each extended upward and forward, while the thumbs and other fingers were tightly closed. At the same time he stuck out his tongue. He was spelling out his new name in the Indian sign language, just to see how it would look.

The boy only held his hands in this position for an instant, and then dropped them to clutch a gun that was slipping from his knees, across which he had laid it. The movement attracted Glen's attention to the gun, and his face flushed angrily as he recognized his own precious rifle, in which he had taken such pride and delight. It was too bad. Then the thought flashed into his mind, would he ever again care for a rifle or anything else in this world? What did Indians do with prisoners? Tortured them, and put them to death, of course. Did not all the stories he had ever read agree on that point? Could it be possible that he, Glen Eddy, was to be tortured, perhaps burned at the stake? Was that what coming out on the Plains meant? Had life with all its hopes and joys nearly ended for him? It could not be! There must be some escape from such a horrible fate! The poor boy gazed about him wildly, but saw only the endless sea of grass stretching to the horizon on all sides, and the stern faces of his captors, one of whom held the end of a lariat that was fastened about the mule's neck.

They all carried bows and arrows slung to their backs, as well as rifles that lay across their knees. They wore moccasins and leggings of buckskin, but no clothing above their waists. Their saddles were simply folded blankets, which would be their covering at night. In place of stirrups they used strips of buffalo hide with a loop at each end. These were thrown across the blanket saddles, and the feet of the riders were supported in the loops. One of them had a pair of field-glasses slung by a strap from his shoulders.

Until nearly noon they pushed westward across

the trackless undulations of the prairie, and Glen became so faint from hunger and thirst, and so stiff from his painful position, that he could hardly retain his seat. His mule was a long-limbed, raw-boned animal, whose gait never varied from an excruciatingly hard trot. Finally, the boy's sufferings reached such a point that it was all he could do to keep from screaming, and he wondered if any torture could be worse.

At length they came to a tiny stream, fringed with a slender growth of willows, and here a long rest was taken. Glen could not stand when his ankles were unbound, and he was allowed to slip from the mule's back, but fell heavily to the ground. The Indian boy said something to his companions, one of whom replied with a grunt, whereupon the lad unbound the prisoner's arms, and helped him to reach the edge of the stream. He was wonderfully revived by plunging his head into the cool water, and the young Indian, who seemed a good-natured sort of a chap, assisted to restore the circulation in his wrists and ankles by rubbing them vigorously. The men smiled scornfully at this; but the boy rubbed away with a hearty good-will, and smiled back at them. He wanted to get this prisoner into the village in as good a condition as possible, and was perfectly willing to be laughed at, if he could only accom-

plish his object. He even went so far as to kin-
dle a small fire of dry, barkless wood, that would
make but little smoke, and heat a strip of dried
buffalo-meat over its coals for the prisoner to eat,
though wondering at a taste that did not find
raw meat just as palatable as cooked. Then he
tried to converse with Glen; but, as the latter
did not understand either Cheyenne or the sign
language, and as the only English word Wolf-
Tongue knew was "How," this attempt proved
a failure.

How Glen wished he could talk with this Indian boy. Why were not white boys taught the
Indian language in school, so as to be prepared
for such emergencies? It would be so much
more valuable than Latin. He wondered if he
would have studied it any harder than he had
other things, if it had been included in the Brimfield High School course. How far away Brimfield seemed! What wouldn't he give to be there
at this moment? How would they feel at home
if they could see him now?

At length it was time to go on again. The
animals, which had been hobbled to prevent them
from straying, left the juicy grasses of the bottom-land with reluctance; and, with a heavy
heart and still aching body, Glen again mounted
his mule. His saddle was the coyote-skin that

had been thrown over his head when he was captured. Now he was given a pair of raw-hide Indian stirrups; while, though his hands were again tied behind his back, his feet were left un-bound. He therefore rode much more comfort-ably now than before, and Wolf-Tongue, who seemed to consider the prisoner as his especial property, was allowed to hold the end of his lariat.

All the movements of these scouts were as care-fully guarded as though they were surrounded by enemies. They avoided soft places where a trail might be left, and whenever they ascended a swell of the prairie they halted just before reaching the top. One of them, dismounting, would then creep cautiously forward, and, with-out exposing his body above the crest, would gaze long and searchingly in every direction. Not until he was satisfied that no human being was within range of his vision would he show himself on the summit, and beckon his comrades to join him.

The afternoon was half gone, when, on one of these occasions, the scout who had just crept to the top of an elevation was seen by the others to gaze long and steadily in a particular direc-tion through his field-glass. At length, appa-rently satisfied with what he saw, he stood up, and flashed a dazzling ray of sunlight from a small mirror that he held in his hand. Again and again did he send that flash over miles of prairie, before he saw the answering flash for which he was watching. Then he called the others up; they talked earnestly together for a few minutes, and, having reached some conclusion, they galloped rapidly away, almost at right angles to the course they had been following.

Glen wondered what this movement meant; but it was not until they had ridden for nearly an hour that his unasked questions were answered. Then, as though by magic, so unexpectedly did they appear, a score or more of Indians seemed to spring from the ground and surround them. It was a Cheyenne war-party. Their ponies, under watchful guard, grazed in a slight depression to one side of them, and their scouts kept a keen lookout from a rise of ground beyond.

While these warriors were exchanging greetings with the new-comers, and regarding the prisoner with unconcealed satisfaction, two white men, utterly unsuspicious of their presence so near them, were lounging in front of the Lost Creek stage station, less than a mile away. From this station the scouts had stolen their ponies and the white mule two nights before.

The ranch and stable stood side by side, and were low, one-story buildings, with walls of a soft sandstone, quarried near by, and roofs of poles covered with sods. Behind them was a corral enclosed by a low stone wall. The ranch and stable were connected by a narrow subterranean passage, and another led from the house to a "dug-out," or square pit, some ten yards from it. This "dug-out" had a roof of poles heavily covered with earth and sods; while, just at the surface of the ground, port-holes opened on all sides. A similar pit, on the other side, could be reached from the stable, and another, in the rear of the station, was connected with the corral.

Lost Creek Station had suffered greatly at the hands of Indians that summer. Its inmates had been killed, and its stock run off. Now but two men were left to guard it. This afternoon they were watching anxiously for the stage from the east, which was some hours overdue.

Suddenly, as they gazed along the distant wagon trail, there came a thunderous rush of hoofs from behind the station. But the men had heard the sound before, and did not need to look to know what it meant.

"They're after us again, Joe!" exclaimed one, in a disgusted tone, as they sprang into the ranch and barred its heavy door behind them. A moment later they were in the "dug-out" behind the corral, and the gleaming barrels of two rifles were thrust from two of its narrow port-holes.

"I swear, Joe! if one of them hasn't the cheek to ride old Snow-ball, and he's in the lead, too. You drop him, and I'll take the next one."

There were two reports. A white mule pitched heavily forward and its rider was flung to the ground. A wounded Indian clung to his pony. Then the whole band wheeled and dashed back to where they had come from, taking both their wounded warrior and the one who had been flung to the ground with them.

"Did you notice that the fellow I dropped had a white man's hat on?" asked Joe, as the two men watched the retreat of their foes.

"Yes, and white men's clothes on, too. I wonder who he murdered and robbed to get 'em?"

Chapter XVII.

A CHEYENNE WAR-PARTY.

THE war-party, detected by the wonderful eye-sight of the Cheyenne scout while they were yet miles away from him, had been for more than a week engaged in attacking stages and wagon-trains on the Smoky Hill Trail. Hiding behind some slight elevation, or in a cottonwood thicket near the road, with keen-eyed scouts always on the lookout, they would burst like a whirlwind on their unsuspecting victims, pour in a withering volley of bullets and arrows, and disappear, almost before a return shot could be fired. Sometimes they would maintain a running fight for miles with a stage, their fleet ponies easily keeping pace with its frantic mules, and many a one thus fell into their hands. Its fate was always the same. If any of its defenders survived the fight they were either killed or reserved for the worse fate of captives. Its mail-sacks were ripped open and their contents scattered far and wide. Finally it was set on fire and destroyed.

Sometimes the stages escaped; in which case

their passengers had marvellous tales to tell. One of these, that reached the safety of General Lyle's wagon-train just in time to avoid capture, had but one living passenger, a woman who was not even wounded during the almost continuous storm of arrows and bullets of a ten-mile running fight. Four dead men, one of whom was her husband, were inside the coach, and another was on the box with the driver. The latter was wounded, and the mules fairly bristled with arrows. The stage itself was shivered and splintered in every part by the shower of lead that had been poured into it, and many a blood-stained letter from its mail-sacks afterwards carried a shudder into distant Eastern homes.

This, then, was the work of the war-party who were gathered about Glen Eddy; and, even now, they were impatiently awaiting the appearance of the stage from the east that was due that day. For this occasion they had planned a new form of attack. It was not to be made until the stage reached the ranch. There, while its mules were being changed, and its occupants were off their guard, the Indians proposed to dash out from the nearest place of concealment and attempt the capture of both it and the station at the same time. It was a well-conceived plan, and might have been successfully carried out, but for the arrival of the three scouts, who were now so proudly exhibiting their prisoner and telling the story of his capture. Before they had half finished, a few dazzling flashes of light from the mirrors of the distant lookouts announced that the eastern stage was in sight.

A minute later the warriors were mounted and riding cautiously towards a point but a short distance from the ranch, where they could still remain concealed from it until the moment of making their final dash. The three scouts, being on other duty, were not expected to take part in the fight, nor had they any intention of so doing, much as they would have liked to; but they could not resist the temptation to witness it. So they, with their prisoner, followed close behind the others to their new place of concealment. When they reached it, these three, with Glen, stood a little apart from the rest, so as not to interfere with their movements.

Up to this moment, the boy had not the least idea of what was about to take place, nor where he was. There was nothing to indicate that a stage ranch and a well-travelled wagon road lay just beyond the ridge before him. He wondered what these Indians were up to; but he wondered still more when they would go into camp, and give him a chance to dismount from the back of that hard-trotting mule; for his aches and pains had again become very hard to bear. In spite of his thoughts being largely centred upon himself, Glen could not help noticing the uneasy movements of his steed, and his impatient snuffings of the air, that began as soon as they came to a halt. The scouts noticed them, too, and watched the mule narrowly.

Suddenly the animal threw up his great head, and in another instant would have announced his presence to all the country thereabout by a sonorous, far-reaching bray. Before he could open his mouth, however, one of the scouts sprang from his pony and seized him by the nose. In the struggle that followed, the end of the lariat held by Wolf-Tongue was jerked from his hand. At the same moment the mule succeeded in shaking off the scout with such violence that he staggered for nearly a rod before recovering his balance. Then, so quickly that Glen was very nearly flung from his back, the animal sprang to the crest of the little ridge, and dashed, with astonishing speed, towards the corral that had been his home for so long, and which he had scented so plainly the moment he reached its vicinity.

Of course the entire body of Indians was in instant pursuit—not of the mule, but of the prisoner that he was bearing from them. Like a thunderclap out of a clear sky, they rushed down that slope, every pony doing his best, and their riders yelling like demons. From the first, Wolf-Tongue took the lead. It was his prisoner who was escaping, his first one. He must have him again. He would almost rather die than lose him. So he lashed his pony furiously with the quirt, or Indian riding-whip of rawhide fastened to his wrist, and leaned far over on his neck, and yelled, and beat the animal's sides with his moccasined feet, until he had gained a lead of all the others and was almost within reach of the mule. Another moment and he would have that trailing lariat in his hand.

Glen, too, was kicking the sides of his ungainly steed, and yelling at him in a perfect frenzy of excitement. He saw the stage ranch, the winding wagon trail, and the shining river beyond the instant he was borne over the crest of the ridge, and knew what they meant for him. To reach that little clump of buildings first, meant life, liberty, and restoration to his friends. He must do it, and he fully believed he could. He leaned as far as possible over the mule's neck, and shouted encouraging words into his ears. What wonderful speed the long-legged animal was showing! Who would have thought it was in him?

"Well done, mule!" yelled Glen. "A few more seconds and we'll be there! They can't catch us now!"

Then came a burst of flame from the earth in front of him. The white mule gave a convulsive bound and fell dead in his tracks, while poor Glen was flung far over his head to the ground, which he struck so heavily as to partially stun him.

Without checking the speed of their ponies in the least, two stalwart warriors bent over, and, seizing the boy by the arms, raised him between them as they swept past. A moment later the entire band, minus only their white mule, had again reached their place of concealment, and poor Glen, breathless, bruised, and heart-broken with disappointment, was more of a prisoner than ever. Besides this, Wolf-Tongue, the only one amid all those stern-featured warriors who had shown the least particle of pity for him, was wounded—a rifle-ball having passed through the calf of one of his legs.

This sudden derangement of his plans caused the leader of the war-party to abandon them altogether, and decide upon a new one. It would be useless to attempt to surprise the stage and station now. Besides, it might be just as well to leave the trail in peace for a few days, in order that the large party of white men, of whom the scouts had just brought information, might come on with less caution than they would use if constantly alarmed. He would send runners to the villages of the Kiowas, Arrapahoes, and Comanches, and tell them of the rich prize awaiting their combined action. In the meantime he would return to his own village and raise a war-party that, in point of numbers and equipment, should be a credit to the great Cheyenne nation.

So the runners were despatched, and the rest of the party set out in a northwesterly direction towards their distant villages on the American Fork.

Shortly before the Indians halted for the night, even Glen almost forgot his heartache and painful weariness of body in the excitement of seeing his first buffalo, and witnessing an Indian buffalo-hunt on a small scale. It was just at sunset, when the scout, who rode ahead, signalled, from the top of an elevation, by waving his blanket in a peculiar manner, that he had discovered buffalo.

Obeying a command from their leader, half a dozen warriors at once dashed ahead of the party; and, joining the scout, disappeared over the ridge. As the others gained the summit, they saw that the plain beyond it was covered with a vast herd of

"TWO STALWART WARRIORS SEIZED HIM BY THE ARMS AND RAISED HIM BETWEEN THEM AS THEY SWEPT PAST"

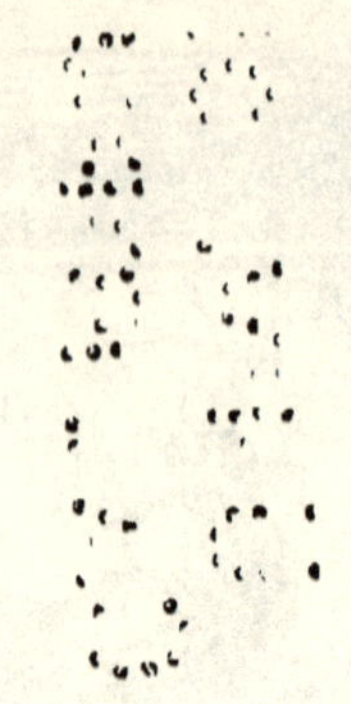

buffalo, quietly feeding, singly or in groups, and spreading over the country as far as the eye could reach. There were thousands of them, and Glen was amazed at the wonderful sight.

Those nearest to the advancing Indians had already taken the alarm, and in less than a minute more the whole vast mass was in motion, with loud bellowings and a lumbering gallop, that, shaking the earth, sounded like the rush and roar of mighty waters. The fleet war-ponies speedily bore the hunters into the thick of the flying mass, so that for a few seconds they were swallowed up and lost to view in it. Then they reappeared surrounding, and driving before them, a fat young cow, that they had cut out from the rest of the herd. They did not use their rifles, as the reports might have attracted undesirable attention to their presence. From their powerful bows arrow after arrow was buried in the body of the selected victim, some of them even passing completely through it, until at length the animal fell, and the chase was ended.

CHAPTER XVIII

BUFFALO AND THEIR USES.

IF the Cheyennes had been on a regular hunt they would have killed scores of the mighty beasts before desisting from their bloody work; but buffalo were too valuable to the Plains Indian to be wasted, or killed for mere sport. In fact, their very existence, at that time, depended upon these animals. Not only did their flesh form the chief and almost the sole article of Indian food, but with the skins they covered their lodges, and made boats, ropes, lariats, trunks, or *par fléche* sacks, saddles, shields, frames for war bonnets, gloves, moccasins, leggings, shirts, guncovers, whips, quivers, knife - scabbards, cradles, saddle-bags and blankets, beds, bridles, boots, glue, and a score of other necessary articles.

From the hair they made ropes and pillows; while the horns provided them with spoons, cups, dishes, powder-flasks, arrow-heads, and even bows. Buffalo sinews gave the Indians thread and twine for innumerable purposes; while certain of the bones were fashioned into axes, knives, arrow-points, and implements for scraping the hides or dressing robes. The ribs were formed into small dog sledges, and the teeth into necklaces and rattles. Buffalo chips were a most important article of fuel on the almost treeless plains, and this is only a partial list of the useful articles furnished to the Indians by this animal. At that time buffalo roamed, in countless thousands, from the Missouri River to the Rocky Mountains, and from Mexico up into British America. Since then they have been ruthlessly slaughtered and exterminated by skin-butchers, emigrants, and an army of so-called sportsmen from all parts of the world.

While the hunters were cutting up the cow they had killed, the rest of the party went into camp on the bank of the stream, near which the vast herd had been feeding. Here Wolf-Tongue's wound, that had only been rudely bandaged to check the flow of blood, was carefully dressed and attended to.

There was no lack of food in the camp that evening, and the warriors were evidently determined to make up for their days of hard riding and fighting on scanty rations, by indulging in a regular feast.

Glen was disgusted to see the liver and kidneys of the buffalo eaten raw, as was also a quantity of the meat while it was yet warm. Still there was plenty of cooked meat for those who preferred it.   Over small fires, carefully screened by robes and blankets, so that their light should not attract attention, ribs were roasted and choice bits were broiled.   Even the prisoner was unbound and allowed to cut and broil for himself until he could eat no more.

Wolf-Tongue's wounded leg was smeared with melted tallow; and, though it was so lame and stiff that he could not use it, his appetite was in no wise impaired by his wound, nor did it dampen his high spirits in the least.   It rather added to them; for, as he ate buffalo meat raw or cooked, as it was handed to him, at the same time laughing and chatting with those of the younger warriors who were nearest his own age, he felt that an honorable wound had been the only thing needed to crown the glories of this, his first warpath.   Now he would indeed be greeted as a hero upon his return to the village.   He felt more assured than ever that he would be allowed to keep the fine name of "Wolf-Tongue."   Perhaps, but it was only just within the range of possibility, the head men might commemorate at once his success as a scout, and the fact that he had received a wound in battle, by conferring upon him the distinguished name of "Lame Wolf."

Such things had been known. Why might they not happen to him?

When the feasting was ended, and the entire band began to feel that to sleep would be far better than to eat any more, they extinguished their fires and moved noiselessly away, a hundred yards or so, from the place where they had been. Here in the tall grass, at the foot of the cotton-wood-trees, or in red willow thickets, the tired warriors laid down, each man where he happened to be when he thought he had gone far enough for safety. Each drew his blanket over his head, and also over the rifle that was his inseparable bedfellow. The ponies had already been securely fastened, so that they could be had when wanted, and now they were either lying down or standing motionless with drooping heads. The camp was as secure as an Indian camp ever is, where every precaution is taken to guard against surprise, except the simple one of keeping awake.

Wolf-Tongue, who was unable to touch his foot to the ground, was carried to his sleeping-place with his arms about the necks of two of his stalwart friends. Now, with Glen's rifle clasped tightly to him, and with his head completely enveloped in a blanket, he was fast forgetting his pain in sleep.

Poor Glen was forced to lie without any blanket,

either over or under him, with his wrists bound together, and with one of his arms fastened, by a short cord, to an arm of one of the scouts who had captured him. The latter fell asleep almost instantly, as was proved by his breathing; but it was impossible for the prisoner, weary as he was, to do so. His mind was too busily engaged in revolving possible means of escape. For a long time he lay with wide-open eyes, dismissing one project after another as they presented themselves. Finally he decided that, unless he could first free his hands and then release his arm from the cord that bound him to the scout, he could do nothing.

To accomplish the first of these objects, he began to gnaw, very softly, at the raw-hide thong by which his wrists were secured. How tough and hard it was. How his jaws ached after he had worked for an hour or more, without accomplishing his purpose. Still he could feel that his efforts were not altogether fruitless. He knew that he could succeed if he were only given time enough.

He was obliged to take several rests, and his work was often interrupted by hearing some wakeful Indian get up and walk about. Twice the scout wakened, and pulled at the cord fastened to his prisoner's arm to assure himself that he was still there.

At length the task was concluded, the hateful thong was bitten in two, and Glen's hands were free. They were cold, numb, and devoid of feeling; but after a while their circulation was gradually restored, and the boy began to work at the knot that secured the cord about his arm. It was a hard one to untie, but in this, too, he finally succeeded. Just as it loosened beneath Glen's fingers, the scout woke and gave the cord a pull. Fortunately the boy still held it, and the other was satisfied that his prisoner was still beside him. Glen hardly dared breathe until he felt certain that the Indian again slept. Then he fastened the cord to a bit of willow, that grew within reach, in order that there might be some resistance if the scout should pull at it again, and cautiously rose to his feet.

Which way should he go? How should he avoid stepping on some recumbent form if he moved at all? For a moment he stood irresolute. Well, whatever he did he must do quickly, for the short summer night was far advanced. He had not a moment to lose. If he only dared take a pony! If he could drive them all off and leave his pursuers without a horse on which to follow him! It was a thought worthy of a Cheyenne scout, and Glen realized in a moment that, hazardous as the undertaking would be, it offered the only means of ultimate escape. He thought he knew where the horses were, and began to move with the utmost caution, feeling his way inch by inch, in that direction.

Twice he just discovered a motionless human form in time to avoid stumbling over it, and each time his heart seemed to leap into his mouth with the narrowness of his escape. Several times, too, he changed his course in order to avoid some real or fancied obstacle, until at length he was completely bewildered, and obliged to confess that he had no idea of what direction he was taking. Still he kept on, trembling with nervousness, until at length he felt certain that he must be at least well outside the circle of sleeping Indians, if not at a considerable distance from them. He began to move more rapidly, when suddenly a human figure rose up before him, so close that he could not avoid it. He sprang at it with a blind fury, hoping to overthrow it, and still effect his escape. Then there came a wild cry, a deafening report, and Glen found himself engaged in a furious struggle with an unknown antagonist.

Chapter XIX.

As Glen struggled desperately, but well-nigh hopelessly, with the assailant who had risen so unexpectedly to bar his escape, there came a crashing volley of shots, a loud cheer, and a rush of trampling feet through the willows and tangled undergrowth. The boy only dimly wondered at these sounds as he was flung to the ground, where he lay breathless, with his arms pinned tightly to the earth, and expecting that each instant would be his last. Then he became strangely conscious that his antagonist was talking in a language that he understood, and was saying,

"Yez would, would ye? An' yez tho't ye could wrastle wid Terence O'Boyle? Ye murtherin' rid villin! Bad cess to it! but oi'll tache ye! Phat's that ye say? Ye're a white man? Oh, no, me omadhoon! yez can't fool me into lettin' ye up that way!"

"But I am white!" cried Glen, half choked though he was. "Let me up, and I'll prove it to you. Can't you understand English?"

Very slowly and reluctantly the astonished Irishman allowed himself to become convinced that the assailant he had failed to shoot, but whom he had overcome after a violent struggle, was not an Indian. It was some minutes before he would permit Glen to rise from his uncomfortable position, and even then he held him fast, declaring that nothing short of an order from the captain himself would induce him to release a prisoner.

The explanation of this sudden change in our hero's fortunes and prospects is that, while the Cheyennes were engaged in their buffalo-hunt the evening before, they had been discovered by a Pawnee scout. He was attached to a company of cavalry who were on their way back to Fort Hayes, on the Smoky Hill, from an expedition against the Arrapahoes. The captain of this company had determined to surprise the Indians thus unexpectedly thrown in his way, at daybreak, and had made his arrangements accordingly. Their movements had been carefully noted by the scouts, and, having made a start from their own camp at three o'clock that morning, the troops were cautiously surrounding the place where they supposed their sleeping foes to be.

The attack would undoubtedly have proved

successful, and the Cheyennes would have sprung from their grassy couches only to fall beneath the fire from the cavalry carbines, had not Glen Eddy run into trooper Terence O'Boyle and been mistaken for an Indian by that honest fellow. Upon the alarm being thus prematurely given, the soldiers fired a volley and charged the Cheyenne camp, only to find it deserted. With one exception, the Indians had made good their escape, and it was never known whether any of them were even wounded by the volley that gave them such a rude awakening. The one who failed to escape was the young scout who hoped to be known as "Wolf-Tongue," and who, on account of his wound, was unable to fly with the rest.

He managed to conceal himself in a thicket until daylight. Then he was discovered by one of the Pawnee scouts, who dragged him out, and would have put him to death but for the interference of Glen Eddy, who was just then led to the spot by his Irish captor.

An hour later Glen was enjoying the happiest breakfast in his life, in company with Captain Garrett Winn, U.S.A., who was listening with absorbed interest to the boy's account of his recent thrilling experiences.

"Well, my lad," said the captain, when Glen had finished his story, "I consider your several escapes from being killed, when first captured, from the bullets of those fellows at the stage ranch, from the Indians, and, finally, from being killed by that wild Irishman, as being little short of miraculous."

Soon afterwards the trumpet sounded " Boots and Saddles," and Glen, mounted on a handsome bay mare—which, with several other ponies, had been left behind by the Indians in their hurried flight—trotted happily away with his new friends in the direction of Fort Hayes. In his hand he grasped his own rifle, which was recovered when Wolf-Tongue was captured, and behind him, mounted on a pony led by one of the troopers, rode that wounded and crest-fallen young Indian himself.

The future looked very black to Wolf-Tongue just now; for, totally ignorant of the ways of white men, he expected nothing less than death as soon as he should reach the fort. He realized that Glen had saved him from the knife of the Pawnee scout, and wondered if the white boy would interfere in his behalf with the warriors of his own race, or if they would listen to him in case he did. He wished he knew just a little of the white man's language, that he might dis-cover what those soldiers on each side of him were talking about. Perhaps they were even discussing him and his fate. But he only knew one word of English, and now he began to think he did not understand the meaning of that; for, though he heard the soldiers say "how" several times in the course of their conversation, they did not seem to use it at all as he would. So the Indian lad rode along unhappily enough; but, though his thoughts were very busy, no trace of them was allowed to exhibit itself in his impassive face.

In the meantime he was the subject of a conversation between Glen and Captain Winn, as they rode side by side. The former had a very kindly feeling towards the young Indian, who had tried to be kind to him when their present positions were reversed, and now he wanted in some way to return this kindness if possible.

"What will be done with him do you think, sir?" he asked.

"I'm sure I don't know," replied the captain, carelessly. "I suppose he will be kept as a prisoner at some one of the forts until we have whipped his tribe and put it on a reservation, and then he will be sent back to it."

"But what will become of him then?" persisted the boy.

"Oh, he will grow up to be one of the regular reservation beggars, living on government charity, until he finally drinks himself to death or gets killed in some quarrel. That's the way with most of them on the reservations. You see they haven't anything else to do, and so they drink and gamble, and kill each other just to pass away the time."

"Don't you suppose he could learn to live like white folks if he had the chance?"

"Yes, I suppose he could. In fact, I know he could, if he had the chance; for these Indian boys are about as bright as they make 'em. But I don't know where he'll get the chance. The government would rather pay a thousand dollars to keep him on a reservation, or even to kill him, than a hundred to give him an education, and I don't know of anybody else, that is able to do anything, who will take an interest in him."

There the conversation ended; for, after riding some time in silence and trying to think of a solution of this perplexing Indian problem, Glen all at once found himself nodding so that he almost fell off his horse. He was so thoroughly wearied and sleepy that it did not seem as though he could hold his eyes open another minute.

Noticing his condition, the captain said, kindly,

"You look just about used up, young man; and no wonder, after what you've gone through. The best thing for you to do is to hand your pony over to one of the men, crawl into the wagon back there, and take a nap."

Glen thought this such good advice that he immediately followed it. Two minutes later he was lying, in what looked like a most uncomfortable position, on top of a pile of baggage in the only wagon that accompanied the troops, more soundly asleep than he had ever been before in all his life. He did not even know when the wagon reached the fort, a few hours later, nor did he realize what was happening when he was lifted from it and led by the captain into his own quarters. There the boy was allowed to tumble down on a pile of robes and blankets, and told to have his sleep out.

Not until the rising sun streamed full in his face the next morning did that sleep come to an end. Then he awoke so hungry that he felt as though it would take a whole buffalo to satisfy his appetite, and so bewildered by his surroundings that, for some minutes, he could not recall what had happened. He had no idea of where he was, for he could remember nothing since the act of crawling into the wagon and finding a bed on its load of baggage.

Chapter XX.

A PRESENT THAT WOULD PLEASE ANY BOY.

THROUGH the open window, by which the sunlight was streaming in, Glen caught a glimpse of a line of cottonwood-trees, which, as he had long ago learned, denoted the presence of a stream in that country. To a boy who dearly loved to bathe, and had not washed for two whole days, nothing could be more tempting. Nor was Glen long in jumping from the window, running down to the cottonwoods, throwing off his clothes, and plunging headforemost into the cool waters.

With that delicious bath disappeared every trace of his weariness, his aches, and everything else that remained to remind him of his recent trials, except his hunger. When he was at length ready to go in search of something with which to appease that, he walked slowly back towards the house in which he had slept. He now noticed that it was built of logs, and was the last one in a row of half a dozen just like it. He also heard bugle calls, saw soldiers in blue uniforms hurrying in every direction, and wisely concluded that, in some way, he must have been brought to Fort Hayes.

As he stood irresolute near the house, not knowing which way to go or what to do, a door opened and a little girl, followed by a lady, came out. The child stopped and looked at the boy for a moment. Then running back to her mother, she exclaimed,

"Look mamma! look! It's the very same one we knew on the cars!"

Glen had recognized her at once as his little acquaintance of the railroad between St. Louis and Kansas City, and now the lady recognized him as the boy who had run the locomotive so splendidly that terrible night, and had then so mysteriously disappeared.

It was truly a very happy party that gathered about Captain Winn's hospitable breakfast-table that morning. They had so much to talk about, and so many questions to ask, and so many experiences to relate, and Nettie so bubbled over with delight at again finding her playfellow, that the meal was prolonged for more than an hour beyond its usual limits.

After breakfast Glen asked if he might go and see the prisoner, to which the captain replied, "Certainly you may." As they walked across the parade-ground in the direction of the guard-house, Glen was introduced to several officers, who seemed to take a great interest in him, and shook hands so cordially, and congratulated him so heartily on his escape from the Cheyennes, that the boy began to think his rough experience was not without its compensations after all.

In the guard-house they found the young Indian peering disconsolately out between the gratings of his cell window, and looking very forlorn indeed. He gazed sullenly at the visitors, and wondered why they should come there to stare at him; but when Glen stepped up to him with outstretched hand, and said "How?" the boy's face brightened at once. He took the proffered hand, and answered "How" with an evident air of pleasure, for he could comprehend the other's sympathetic expression, if he could not understand his language. Pointing to himself, the white boy said, "Glen," which the other repeated as though he thoroughly understood what was meant. Then Glen pointed to him, with an inquiring look, as much as to ask, "What is your name?"

The boy understood; but hesitated a moment before drawing himself up proudly and answering in his own tongue; but the name was so long and hard to say that Glen could not repeat it.

"I wish I could understand what he says, for I should so like to have a talk with him," said Glen.

"There is an interpreter who speaks Cheyenne somewhere about the place," answered Captain Winn, "and, if you like, I will send for him."

When the interpreter came, Glen found out that what the boy had said in Cheyenne was that his name was "Lame Wolf;" but when the young Indian tried to repeat it in English, after Glen, he pronounced it "Lem Wolf," which is what he was called from that day.

After they had held quite a conversation, that greatly increased Glen's interest in the boy, he and the captain took their departure, the former promising to come again very soon.

Then Captain Winn led Glen down to the corral, in which were a number of horses, ponies, and mules, and, pointing to one of them, asked the boy if he recognized it.

"Of course I do," answered Glen. "It's the one I rode yesterday."

"And the one I hope you will ride for many days to come," said the captain with a smile; "for I want you to accept that pony as a present from my little girl."

"Really?" cried the delighted boy; "do you

really mean that I am to have it for my very own?"

"I really do," laughed the captain, "and," he continued more soberly, "I wish I could offer you something ten times more valuable, as a slight memento of the service you rendered those so dear to me not long ago."

"You couldn't give me anything I should value more," exclaimed Glen, "unless—" Here he hesitated, and his face flushed slightly.

"Unless what?" asked Captain Winn.

"Unless you could give me that Indian boy."

"What on earth would you do with him?" cried the captain, his eyes opening wide with surprise at such an unheard-of request.

Then Glen unfolded a plan that had formed itself in his mind within a few minutes; and, when he had finished, the captain's look of surprise still remained on his face, but he said, reflectively:

"Well, I don't know but what it might be done, and if you succeed in carrying out your part of the scheme, I will see what I can do with the rest of it."

This matter being disposed of, Glen asked if he might try his pony.

"But you tried her yesterday," laughed the

captain, who enjoyed the boyishness of this boy as much as he admired his manliness.

" Yes, sir ; but she wasn't mine then, and you know everything, even a horse, is very different when it is your own."

" So it is, and you may try her to your heart's content, only don't ride far from the post unless you wish for a repetition of your recent experience."

With this the captain beckoned to a soldier, who stood near by, and ordered him to saddle the bay mare, and to tell the stable-sergeant that she belonged to this young gentleman, who was to take her whenever he pleased. He also told Glen that the whole outfit of saddle, bridle, and picket rope, then being placed on the mare, were included in his present.

The mare was so well fed, and so thoroughly rested, that she was in high spirits ; and, the moment she found Glen on her back, tried her very best to throw him off. She reared, and bucked, and plunged, and sprang sideways, and kicked up her heels, to the great delight of a number of soldiers who were witnesses of the performance; but all to no purpose. Her rider clung to the saddle like a burr, and all her efforts to throw him were quite as unsuccessful as those of Binney Gibbs's mule had been some days before.

When Glen, with the breath nearly shaken out of his body, but thoroughly master of the situation, reined the mare up beside the captain, and asked his permission to name her " Nettle," the latter readily granted it, saying, " I think it will be a most appropriate name; for it is evident that she can only be mastered by a firm and steady hand."

Then the happy boy rode over to Captain Winn's quarters, anxious to display his new acquisition to the child after whom she had just been named. As he did so he passed the guard-house, and was moved to pity by the sight of a sad-looking young face pressed against the grating of one of its windows, and gazing wistfully at him. That pony had belonged to Lame Wolf but the day before.

After an hour's riding in the immediate vicinity of the fort, Glen was fully satisfied that no horse in the world had ever combined so many admirable qualities as this bay mare, or given an owner such complete cause to be satisfied with his possession.

As he was about to return her to the corral, his eye caught the gleam of sunlight on a moving white object, a mile or so distant, along the wagon-trail leading to the east. Watching intently, he saw that it was followed by another, and another, until the wagons of a long train were in plain sight, winding slowly along the road towards the fort. When he was certain that he could not be mistaken, the boy uttered a joyous shout, clapped spurs to Nettle, and dashed away to meet them.

A group of mounted men rode ahead of the train, and they gazed wonderingly at the reckless rider who approached them with such headlong impetuosity. Their surprise became incredulous amazement as he reined sharply up within a few paces of them, and, politely lifting his hat, disclosed the shaven head and flushed face of the boy whose mysterious disappearance had caused them such sincere grief and distress. They had devoted half a day to scouring the country near the camp from which he had been lost; and, finding plentiful traces of Indians in the creek bottom, had come to the conclusion that, in some way, he had fallen into their hands, and would never again be heard from. Now, to meet him here, safe, and evidently in high spirits, was past comprehension.

Mr. Hobart was the first to ride forward and grasp his hand. "Is it really you, Glen?" he exclaimed, his voice choked with feeling; "and where, in the name of all that is mysterious, have you been?"

"It is really I," answered the boy, "and I've

been a prisoner in the hands of the Cheyennes, and had a glorious time."

It really did seem as though he had had a good time, now that it was all over with, and he was the owner of that beautiful mare. Besides, he could not fully realize the nature of the fate he had escaped.

Then the others crowded about him, and General Lyle himself shook hands with him, and wanted to hear his story at once. While he was telling it as briefly as possible, the joyful news of his appearance flew back through the train, and the boys came running up to see him, and shake hands with him, and nearly pulled him off his horse in their eagerness to touch him and assure themselves that he was really alive.

"Hurrah for the Baldheads!" shouted the irrepressible Brackett; "they don't get left! not much!"

Even Binney Gibbs came and shook hands with him.

That evening, after the camp was somewhat quieted from its excitement, and after Glen had told his story for about the twentieth time, he disappeared for a short while. When he returned he brought with him an Indian boy, who limped painfully, and seemed very ill at ease in the presence of so many strange pale-faces.

" Who's your friend, Glen ?"

" Where are the rest of the ten little Injuns ?" shouted the fellows as they crowded about this new object of interest.

When at length a partial quiet was restored, Glen begged them to listen to him for a few minutes, as he had something to propose that he was sure would interest them, and they shouted,

" Fire away, old man, we are all listening !"

Chapter XXI.

LAME WOLF, THE YOUNG CHEYENNE.

"Look here, fellows," said Glen, as he stood with one hand on the shoulder of the young Indian, and facing his companions, who, attracted by curiosity, were gathered to hear what he had to say. "This chap is a Cheyenne, and is one of the three by whom I was captured; but he was mighty kind, and did everything he could think of to make things easy for me. So you see he is my friend, and now that he is in trouble, I am bound to do what I can to help him. His name is Lame Wolf—" (here the young Indian stood a little straighter, and his eyes flashed. He had succeeded in having that name recognized as belonging to him, at any rate), "and he's the son of a chief, and the only English word he knows is 'How?' Captain Winn says that if he only had a chance he'd learn as quick as any white boy, and I believe he'd learn a good deal quicker than some—" At this point Glen became somewhat confused, and wondered if Binney Gibbs had told how he had been dropped from his class. "He says, I mean Captain Winn says, that the only thing for him to do out here is to go on a reservation and become a worthless good-for-nothing, and get killed. Now that seems a pretty poor sort of a chance for a fellow that's been as good a friend to me as Lame Wolf has, and I want you to help me give him a better one.

"I want to send him back to my home in Brimfield, and let him live with my folks a year or two, and be taught things the same as white boys, and have the same chance they have. Captain Winn says he thinks he can fix it with the folks at Washington about letting him go; but he don't know where the money to pay his expenses is to come from. I didn't tell him, because I thought I'd speak to you first; but I was pretty sure it would come from this very party. I've only got five dollars in cash myself, but I'll give that, and I'll save all I can out of my pay for it, too. Now, what do you say, fellows? Shall Lame Wolf have a chance or not?"

"Yes! yes! of course he shall! Hurrah for Lame Wolf! Hurrah for Glen's little Injun! Give him a chance! Put me down for half a month's pay! And me! and me!" shouted a dozen voices at once.

"Billy" Brackett jumped up on a box, and, calling the meeting to order, proposed that a committee of three be appointed, with Mr. Hobart as its chairman, to receive subscriptions to the Lame Wolf Fund. " All-in-favor-say-aye-contrary-mind-it-is-a-vote!" he shouted. Then somebody else nominated him and Glen to be the other members, and they were elected without a dissenting voice.

While all this was going on the fellows were crowding about the young Indian, eager to shake hands with him, and say, " How! Lame Wolf, old boy ! How !"

All at once Glen found that the boy was leaning heavily on him, and reproached himself for having allowed him to stand so long on his wounded leg. He got his charge back to the guard - house as quickly as possible, and then, leaving him to enjoy a quiet night's rest, hurried back to camp.

Here he found " Billy " Brackett presiding, with great dignity, over what he was pleased to call the " subscription books." They consisted of a single sheet of paper, fastened with thumb-tacks to a drawing-board that was placed on top of a barrel in one of the tents. Mr. Hobart, who had consented to serve on the committee, was also in the tent, and to him were being handed the cash contributions to the Fund.

Glen put his name down for five dollars a month, to be paid as long as he should remain a member of the present expedition. Then he started for his own tent to get the five dollars in cash that he had promised, out of his valise.

As he was hurrying back with it he was stopped by Binney Gibbs, who thrust a bit of paper into his hand, saying,

" I want you to take this check for your Indian, Glen. Father sent it to me to buy a horse with, but I guess a mule is good enough for me, and so the Indian chap can have it as well as not. You needn't say anything about it."

With this, Binney, who had spoken in a confused manner, hurried away without giving Glen a chance to thank him.

What had come over the boy? Glen had never known him to do a generous thing before. He could not understand it. When he reached the tent, and examined the check, his amazement was so great that he gave a long whistle.

" What is it, Glen? Give us a chance to whistle too," shouted " Billy " Brackett. " Our natural curiosity needs to be checked as well as yours."

" Binney Gibbs has contributed a hundred dollars," said Glen, slowly, as though he could not quite believe his own words to be true.

" Good for Grip! Bravo for Binney! Who

would have thought it? He's a trump, after all!" shouted "Billy" Brackett and the others who heard this bit of news.

Far beyond the tent, these shouts reached the ears of a solitary figure that stood motionless and almost invisible in the night shadows. They warmed his heart, and caused his cheeks to glow. It was a new sensation to Binney Gibbs to be cheered and praised for an act of generosity. It was a very pleasant one as well, and he wondered why he had never experienced it before.

The truth is that this rough life, in which every person he met was his equal, if not his superior, was doing this boy more good than any one had dared to predict that it would. Although he was a prize scholar, and the son of a wealthy man, there were many in this exploring-party who were far better scholars, and more wealthy than he. Yet even these were often outranked in general estimation by fellows who had neither social position, money, nor learning. At first Binney could not understand it. Things were so different in Brimfield; though even there he remembered that he had not been as popular among the other boys as Glen Eddy. Even in this party, where Binney had expected to be such a shining light, the other Brimfield boy was far better liked than he. For this Binney had hated

Glen, and declared he would get even with him. Then he began, furtively, to watch him in the hope of discovering the secret of his popularity. Finally it came to him, like a revelation, and he realized for the first time in his life that, in man or boy, such things as unselfishness, honesty, bravery, good-nature, generosity, and cheerfulness, or any one of them, will do more towards securing the regard, liking, and friendship of his fellows than all the wealth or book-learning in the world.

Perhaps if Glen had not been captured by the Cheyennes, Binney would not have learned this most valuable lesson of his life as quickly as he did. In the general grief over his schoolmate's disappearance, he heard his character praised for one or another lovable trait, until at length the secret of Glen's popularity was disclosed to him. Then, as he looked back and recalled the incidents of their Brimfield life, he realized what a manly, fearless, open-hearted boy this one, whom he had regarded with contempt, because he was not a student, had been. Now that he was gone, and, as he supposed, lost to him forever, Binney thought there was nothing he would not give for a chance to recall the past and win the friendship he had so contemptuously rejected.

For two days these thoughts exercised so

strong a sway on Binney's mind, that when, on
the third, Glen Eddy appeared before him as one
risen from the dead, their influence was not to be
shaken off. Although he did not know exactly
how to begin, he was determined not only to win
the friendship of the boy whom he had for so
long regarded as his rival, but also to make every
member of the party like him, if he possibly could.

His first opportunity came that evening; but
it was not until after a long struggle with selfish-
ness and envy that he resolved to contribute that
one-hundred-dollar check to the Lame Wolf Fund.
He knew that he cut an awkward figure on his
mule, and imagined that a horse would not only
be much more elegant, but easier to ride. Then,
too, Glen had such a beautiful mare; beside her
his wretched mule would appear to a greater disadvantage than ever. He could buy as fine a
pony as roamed the Plains for a hundred dollars.
Then, too, that was what his father had sent him
the money for. Had he a right to use it for any
other purpose? To be sure, Mr. Gibbs had not
known of the mule, and supposed his son would
be obliged to go on foot if he did not buy a
horse.

So poor Binney argued with himself, and his
old evil influences strove against the new resolves. It is doubtful if the latter would have

conquered, had not the sight of Glen coming towards him brought a sudden impulse to the aid of the resolves and decided the struggle in their favor.

Thus generosity won, but by so narrow a margin that Binney could not stand being thanked for it, and so hurried away. But he heard the shouts and cheers coupled with his name, and it seemed to him that he felt even happier at that moment than when he stood on the platform of the Brimfield High School and was told of the prize his scholarship had won.

So the money was raised to redeem one young Cheyenne from the misery and wickedness of a government Indian reservation; and, when the grand total of cash and subscriptions was footed up, it was found to be very nearly one thousand dollars. Glen was overjoyed at the result, and it is hard to tell which boy was the happier, as he crept into his blankets that night, he or Binney Gibbs.

Chapter XXII.

THE next day, when Glen announced the successful result of his efforts to Captain Winn, that officer informed him that he expected to be ordered East very shortly on special duty, when he would be willing to take charge of the Indian boy, and deliver him to Mr. Matherson in Brimfield. Nothing could have suited Glen's plans better; and he at once wrote a long letter to his adopted father, telling him of all that had happened, and begging him to receive the young Indian for his sake. He also wrote to Mr. Meadows and asked him to announce the coming of the stranger to the Brimfield boys. Then he hunted up the interpreter, and went to the guard-house for a long talk with his captive friend.

Lame Wolf was glad to see him, and at once asked what the white men had talked of in their council of the evening before. Glen explained it all as clearly as he knew how. The young Indian was greatly comforted to learn that he was not to be put to death, but also seemed to think that it would be nearly as bad to be sent far away from his own country and people, to the land of the Pale-faces. In his ignorance he regarded the place of his proposed exile much as we do the interior of Africa or the North Pole, one only to be reached by a weary journey, that few ever undertook, and fewer still returned from.

He was somewhat cheered by Glen's promise to join him at the end of a year, and that then, if he chose, he should certainly return to his own people. Still, it was a very melancholy and forlorn young Indian who shook hands, for the last time, with the white boy at sunrise the next morning, and said, "How, Glen," in answer to the other's cheery "Good-by, Lame Wolf. Take care of yourself, and I hope you will be able to talk English the next time I see you."

Then, after bidding good-bye to the Winns and his other friends of the post, the boy sprang on Nettle's back and dashed after the wagon-train that was just disappearing over a roll of the prairie to the westward.

All that morning Glen's attention was claimed by Mr. Hobart, or "Billy" Brackett, or somebody else, who wished to learn more of the details of his recent experience; but late in the afternoon he found himself riding beside Binney Gibbs. For the first time in their lives the two boys held a long and earnest conversation. From it each learned of good qualities in the other that he had never before suspected; and by it a long step was taken towards the cementing of a friendship between them.

So engaged were they in this talk, that the animals they were riding were allowed insensibly to slacken their pace, until they had fallen a considerable distance behind the train. They even stopped to snatch an occasional mouthful of grass from the wayside, without opposition on the part of their young riders. These knew that, whenever they chose, a sharp gallop of a minute or two would place them alongside of the wagons, and so they carelessly permitted the distance between them and the train to become much greater than it should have been.

Suddenly a dazzling ray of light flashed, for the fraction of a second, full in Glen's eyes, causing him to start, as though a pistol had been fired close beside him. He glanced hurriedly about. Not a wagon was in sight; but he knew the train must be just over the rise of ground he and Binney were ascending. At that same moment the mule threw up its head and sniffed the air uneasily. Glen's second glance was behind him, and it revealed a sight that, for an instant, stopped the beating of his heart. The whole country seemed alive with Indians.

Half a mile in the rear, hundreds of them, in a dense body, were advancing at the full speed of their ponies. A small party, evidently of scouts, were coming down the slope of a divide at one side, in the direction of the mirror-flash that had first attracted his attention. But the worst danger of all lay in two fierce-looking warriors who had advanced upon the boys so silently and rapidly that they were already within bow-shot.

Fortunately, Glen was close beside his companion. With a quick movement he grasped Binney by the collar and jerked him to one side, so that he very nearly fell off his mule. At the same instant the two arrows, that he had seen fitted to their bowstrings, whizzed harmlessly over the boys' heads. As Nettle and the mule sprang away up the slope, several rifle-balls, from the little party of Indians on the right, whistled past them; while from behind them rose a howl of mingled rage and disappointment. The first two Indians had used the noiseless arrows, in the hope of killing the boys without betraying their presence to the rest of the party, as the moment for the grand charge, that they hoped would be such a complete and overwhelming surprise, had not yet arrived. Now that they had failed in this, there was no longer any need for caution, and they fired shot after shot from their rifles after the fugitives.

Glen had seen the Cheyennes dodge from side to side, as they rode away from the stage-ranch three days before, to disconcert the aim of its defenders; and now he and Binney employed the same device.

Nettle was so much fleeter than the mule that Glen could have gained the top of the slope in advance of his companion if he had so chosen; but he rather chose to be a little behind him at this point. So, instead of urging the mare to do her best, he faced about in his saddle and returned the rifle-shots of the two Indians who were nearest, until his magazine was emptied. It is not likely that any of his shots took effect; but they certainly weakened the ardor of the pursuit, and gave Binney Gibbs a chance to cross the ridge in safety, which he probably could not have done had not Glen held those Indians in momentary check.

With his last shot expended, and no chance to reload, it was evidently high time for Glen to test the speed of his mare to its utmost. His life depended wholly on her now, and he knew it.

There would be no taking of prisoners this time. Even at this critical moment he reflected grimly, and with a certain satisfaction, upon the difficulty the Indians would find in getting a scalp off of his shaven head.

All this riding and shooting and thinking had been done so rapidly that it was not two minutes from the time of that first tell-tale mirror-flash before Nettle had borne her rider to the top of the ridge, and he could see the wagon-train, not a quarter of a mile from him.

Binney Gibbs was already half-way to it; and, as Glen caught sight of him, he was amazed at a most extraordinary performance. Binney suddenly flew from his saddle, not over his mule's head, as though the animal had flung him, but sideways, as though he had jumped. Whether he left the saddle of his own accord or was flung from it the effect was the same; and the next instant he was sprawling at full length on the soft grass, while the mule, relieved of his weight, was making better time than ever towards the wagons.

Glen had left the trail, thinking to cut off a little distance by so doing; and, a few moments after Binney's leap into the air, he performed almost the same act. On his part it was entirely involuntary, and was caused by one of Nettle's fore-feet sinking into a gopher burrow that was invisible and not to be avoided.

As horse and boy rolled over together, a cry of dismay came from one side, and a wild yell of exultation from the other.

Chapter XXIII.

FIGHTING THE FINEST HORSEMEN IN THE WORLD.

It did not take many seconds for both Glen
and Nettle to scramble to their feet after the
tremendous header caused by the gopher - hole.
Badly shaken though he was, the boy managed
to regain his saddle more quickly than he had
ever done before. But seconds are seconds;
and, in so close a race for the most valuable of
all earthly prizes, each one might be worth a
minute, an hour, or even a lifetime. Glen had
not more than regained his seat, before the foremost of his pursuers, who had far outstripped
the other, was upon him. With an empty rifle,
Glen had not the faintest hope of escape this
time, though Nettle sprang bravely forward. He
involuntarily cringed from the expected blow,
for he had caught a fleeting glimpse of an up-
lifted tomahawk; but it did not come. Instead
of it, he heard a crash, and turned in time to see
the Indian pony and its rider pitch headlong, as
he and Nettle had done a minute before. They
were almost beside him; and, as he dashed away,

he was conscious of wondering if they too had fallen victims to an unseen gopher-hole.

He had not noticed the figure running to meet him, nor heard one of the shots it was firing so wildly as it ran. If he had he might have realized that his salvation had not depended on a gopher-hole, but on one of those random shots from Binney Gibbs's rifle. By the merest chance, for it was fired without aim and almost without direction, it had pierced the brain of the Indian pony, and decided that race in favor of Glen.

When, to Glen's great surprise, the two boys met, he sprang from Nettle's back and insisted that Binney should take his place, which the other resolutely refused to do. So Glen simply tossed the bridle rein into Binney's hand, and started off on a full run. In a moment Nettle, with Binney on her back, had overtaken him, and the generous dispute might have been resumed had not a party of mounted men from the wagon-train just then dashed up and surrounded the boys. They were headed by " Billy " Brackett, who cried out,

" Well, you're a pretty pair of babes in the woods, aren't you ? And you've been having lots of fun at the expense of our anxiety ! But jump up behind me, Glen, quick, for I believe every wild Injun of the Plains is coming down that hill after us at this moment."

Just before the first shots were heard, some anxiety had been felt in the train concerning the boys who had lagged behind, and "Billy" Brackett had already asked if he had not better look them up. Then, as the sound of firing came over the ridge, and the boys were known to have got into some sort of trouble, he rode back at full speed, followed by a dozen of the men. All were equally ready to go, but the rest were ordered to remain behind for the protection of the train. Then the wagons were quickly drawn up in double line, and the spare stock was driven in between them.

These arrangements were hardly completed before "Billy" Brackett and his party, with the two rescued boys, came flying back, pursued by the entire body of Indians. As the former gained the wagons they faced about, and, with a rattling volley, checked for an instant the further advance of the dusky pony riders.

But those Cheyennes and Arrapahoes and Kiowas and Comanches were not going to let so rich a prize as this wagon-train and all those scalps escape them without at least making a bold try for it. If they could only force the train to go into corral, while it was a mile away

16

from the nearest stream, they would have taken a long step towards its capture.

So they divided into two bands; and, circling around, came swooping down on the train from both sides at once. The Plains Indians are the finest horsemen in the world, and their everyday feats of daring in the saddle would render the performance of the best circus-riders tame by comparison. Now, as the two parties swept obliquely on towards the motionless wagons, with well-ordered ranks, tossing arms, waving plumes and fringes, gaudy with vivid colors, yelling like demons, and sitting their steeds like centaurs, they presented a picture of savage warfare at once brilliant and terrible.

At the flash of the white men's rifles every Indian disappeared as though shot, and the next moment their answering shower of bullets and arrows came from under their horses' necks. The headlong speed was not checked for an instant; but after delivering their volley they circled off beyond rifle-shot for a breathing-spell.

As they did so, the wagon-train moved ahead. A few mules had been killed and more wounded by the Indian volley; but their places were quickly filled from the spare stock. By the time the Indians were ready for their second charge, the train was several hundred yards nearer the coveted water than before.

Again they halted. Again the young engineers, inwardly trembling with excitement, but outwardly as firm as rocks, took their places under and behind the wagons, with their shining rifle-barrels steadily pointed outward. Some of them had been soldiers, while others had encountered Indians before; but to most of them this was the first battle of any kind they had ever seen. But they all knew what their fate would be if overpowered, and they had no idea of letting these Indians get any nearer than within good rifle-shot.

"If you can't see an Indian, aim at the horses!" shouted General Lyle, from his position on horseback midway between the two lines of wagons. "Don't a man of you fire until I give the word, and then give them as many shots as possible while they are within range."

The chief had not the remotest thought of allowing his train to be captured, nor yet of being compelled to corral it before he was ready to do so.

The second charge of the Indians was even bolder than the first, and they were allowed to come much nearer before the order to fire was given. The same manœuvres were repeated as before. One white man, a member of Mr. Hobart's division, was killed outright, and two others were wounded. More mules were killed than before, and more were injured; but still the train moved ahead, and this time its defenders could see the sparkle of water in the river they longed so ardently to reach. How thirsty they were getting, and what dry work fighting was! The wagon mules sniffed the water eagerly, and could hardly be restrained from rushing towards it.

But another charge must be repelled first. This time it was so fierce that the Indians rode straight on in the face of the first and second volleys from the engineers' rifles. When the third, delivered at less than two rods' distance, finally shattered their ranks, and sent them flying across the level bottom-land, they left a dozen wagon mules transfixed with their lances.

The Indians left many a pony behind them when they retreated from that charge; but in every case their riders, killed, wounded, or unhurt, were borne off by the others, so that no estimate of their loss could be formed.

Before another charge could be made, the wagons had been rushed forward, with their mules on a full gallop, to a point so close to the river-bank that there was no longer any danger of being cut off from it. Here they were corralled, and chained together in such a manner as to present an almost impregnable front to the Indians. At least it was one that those who viewed it, with feelings of bitter disappointment, from a safe distance, did not care to attack. After they had noted the disposition of the train, and satisfied themselves that it was established in that place for the night, they disappeared so completely that no trace of them was to be seen, and the explorers were left to take an account of the losses they had sustained in this brief but fierce encounter.

Only one man killed! What a comfort it was that no more had shared his fate, and yet how sad that even this one should be taken from their number! Glen had known him well; for he was one of those merry young Kansas City surveyors, one of the " bald heads," as they were known in the party. An hour before he had been one of the jolliest among them. He was one of those who had gone out so cheerfully with " Billy " Brackett to the rescue of the boys. He had been instantly killed while bravely doing his duty, and had suffered no pain. They had that consolation as they talked of him in low, awed tones. His body could not be sent home. It could not be carried with them. So they buried him in a grave dug just inside the line of wagons.

The last level beams of the setting sun streamed full on the spot as the chief-engineer read the solemn burial service, and each member of the expedition, stepping forward with uncovered head, dropped a handful of earth into the open grave. Then it was filled, and its mound was beaten to the level of the surrounding surface. After that, mules and horses were led back and forth over it, until there was no longer any chance of its recognition, or disturbance by Indians or prowling beasts.

None of the wounded suffered from severe injuries; and, though the bodies of the wagons were splintered in many places, and their canvas covers gaped with rents, no damage had been sustained that could not be repaired.

Chapter XXIV.

CROSSING THE QUICKSANDS.

As soon as Glen found a chance to talk to Binney Gibbs he asked him how his mule happened to throw him in such a peculiar fashion.

"He didn't throw me," answered Binney, with a look of surprise; "I jumped off."

"What on earth did you do that for?"

"Because he was running away, and I couldn't stop him. I saw that your pony couldn't keep up with him, and, of course, I wasn't going to leave you behind to fight all those Indians alone. So I got off the only way I could think of, and started back to help you. It was mighty lucky I did, too. Don't you think so?"

"Indeed I do!" answered Glen, heartily, though at the same time he could not help smiling at the idea of Nettle not being able to keep up with Binney's mule. He would not for the world, though, have belittled the other's brave act by saying that he had purposely remained behind to cover his companion's flight. He only said, "Indeed I do, and it was one of the finest things

I ever heard of, Binney. I shall always remember it, and always be grateful for it. You made a splendid shot, too, and I owe my life to it; for that Indian was just lifting his hatchet over my head when you rolled him over. I tell you it was a mighty plucky thing for anybody to do, especially—" Glen was about to say, "especially for a fellow who has never been considered very brave;" but he checked himself in time, and substituted, "for a fellow who never had any experience with Indians before."

Binney knew well enough, though, that the Brimfield boys had always thought him a coward; for they had never hesitated to tell him so. Now, to be praised for bravery, and that by the bravest boy he had ever known, was a new and very pleasant sensation. It was even better than to be called generous, and he mentally vowed, then and there, never again to forfeit this newly gained reputation.

There is nothing that will so stimulate a boy or girl to renewed efforts as a certain amount of praise where it is really deserved. Too much praise is flattery; and praise that is not deserved is as bad as unjust censure.

While the boys were thus talking they received word that General Lyle wished to see them. They found him sitting, with Mr. Hobart, in an ambulance; for it had been ordered that no tents should be pitched in that camp. When they stood before the chief-engineer he said, kindly:

"Boys, I want both to reprimand and thank you. I am surprised that you should have so disobeyed my positive orders as to lose sight of the train when on a march through an Indian country. This applies to you, Matherson, more than to your companion; for your late experience should have taught you better. I trust that my speaking to you now will prevent any repetition of such disobedience. Your carelessness of this afternoon might have cost many precious lives, including your own. That is all of the reprimand. The thanks I wish to express are for your timely warning of the presence of Indians, and for the individual bravery displayed by both of you during our encounter with them. That is all I have to say this time, and I hope next time the reprimand may be omitted."

As the two boys, feeling both ashamed and pleased, bowed and took their departure, the chief, turning to his companion, said: "They are fine young fellows, Hobart, and I congratulate you on having them in your division. Now let us decide on our plans for to-night."

This last remark referred to the decision General Lyle had formed of placing the river between his party and the Indians before daylight. He knew that the Indians of the Plains, like all others of their race, are extremely averse to undertaking anything of importance in the dark. He also knew that their favorite time for making an attack is when they can catch their enemy at a disadvantage, as would be the case while his wagons were crossing the river and his men and animals were struggling with its probable quicksands. Another serious consideration was that, during the summer season, all the rivers of the Plains are liable to sudden and tremendous freshets, that often render them impassable for days. Thus it was unwise to linger on the near bank of one that was fordable a moment longer than necessary. He had, therefore, decided to make the crossing of this stream that night, as quietly as possible, and as soon as darkness had set in. For this reason none of the baggage, except the mess-chests and a sack of corn, had been taken from the wagons, so that a start could be made at a few minutes' notice.

With the last of the lingering daylight the chief, accompanied by Mr. Hobart and the wagon-master, crossed the river on horseback, to discover its depth, the character of its bottom, the nature of the opposite bank, and to locate a camping-ground on its farther side. They found the water to be but a few inches deep, except in one narrow channel, where it had a depth of about three feet. They also found the bottom to be of that most treacherous of quicksands which is so hard that a thousand-pound hammer cannot force a post into it, yet into which that same post would slowly sink of its own weight until lost to sight, and held with such terrible tenacity that nothing short of a steam-engine could pull it out. Such a quicksand as this is not dangerous to the man or animal who keeps his feet in constant motion while crossing it, but woe to him if he neglects this precaution for a single minute. In that case, unless help reaches him, he is as surely lost as though clasped in the relentless embrace of a tiger.

The only place on the opposite bank where teams could emerge from the water was very narrow, and a team striking below it in the dark would almost certainly be lost. Thus the problem of a safe crossing at night became a difficult one. It would be unsafe to build fires or use lanterns, as these would surely draw the attention, and probably the bullets, of the Indians.

Finally the plan was adopted of stretching a rope across the river, from bank to bank, on the lower side of the ford, with a line of men stationed along its entire length, so that no team could get below it. These were charged, as they valued their lives, to keep their feet in constant motion, and on no account to let go of the rope.

First the ambulances were put across. Then the spare stock and saddle-animals were led over, and securely fastened. Six spare mules, harnessed and attached to a loose rope, were held in readiness, on the farther bank, to assist any team that might get stalled in the river. Then, one by one, the heavily laden wagons began to cross, with two men leading each team. There was little difficulty except at the channel, where the mules were apt to be frightened at the sudden plunge into deeper water.

A mule hates the dark almost as much as an Indian; he dislikes to work in water, and above all he dreads miry places or quicksands, for which his small, sharp hoofs are peculiarly unfitted. He is easily panic-stricken, and is then wholly unmanageable. A team of mules, finding themselves stalled in a stream, will become frantic with terror. They utter agonized cries, attempt to clamber on one another's back, and frequently drown themselves before they can be cut loose from the traces and allowed to escape.

In spite of all the difficulties to be overcome, the wagons were got safely over, until only one remained, and it had started on its perilous journey. Those members of the party who stood in the water holding the rope were becoming thoroughly chilled, as well as wearied by the tread-mill exercise necessary to keep their feet from sinking in the quicksand. Thus, though they still stuck manfully to their posts, they were thankful enough that this was the last wagon, and noted the sound of its progress with eager interest. They were all volunteers, for nobody had been ordered to remain in the river, and this fact added to the strength of purpose with which they maintained their uncomfortable positions.

Among them were Glen Eddy and Binney Gibbs, who, when volunteers were called for to perform this duty, had rushed into the river among the first. Now they stood, side by side, near the middle of the stream, and close to the edge of the channel. They rejoiced to see the dim bulk of the last wagon looming out of the darkness, and to know that their weary task was nearly ended.

The mules of this team were unusually nervous, splashing more than any of the others had done, and snorting loudly. The rope had been cast loose from the bank the party had so recently quitted, and all those who had upheld it beyond Glen and Binney had passed by them on their way to the other side. They, too, would be relieved from duty as soon as the team crossed the channel.

But there seemed to be some difficulty about persuading the mules to cross it. As the leaders felt the water growing deeper and the sandy bank giving way beneath them, they sprang back in terror, and threw the whole team into confusion. The wagon came to a standstill, and everybody in the vicinity realized its danger. The driver, feeling that the need for silence and caution was past, began to shout at his mules, and the reports of his blacksnake whip rang out like pistol-shots.

In the excitement of the moment nobody noticed or paid any attention to a gleaming line of white froth that came creeping down the river, stretching from bank to bank like a newly formed snow-drift. Suddenly a rifle-shot rang out from the bank they had left, then another, and then a dozen at once. The Indians had discovered their flight, and were firing angrily in the direction of the sounds in the river. The teamster sprang from his saddle, and, cutting the traces of his mules, started them towards the shore, leaving the wagon to its fate.

"It's time we were off, too, old man," said Glen, as he started to follow the team.

"I can't move, Glen! Oh, help me! I'm sinking !" screamed Binney, in a tone of inexpressible anguish.

Glen dropped the rope, and sprang to his companion's assistance.

At the same instant there came a great shout from the bank, " Hurry up, there's a freshet coming! Hurry! Hurry, or you'll be swept away!"

With both arms about Binney, Glen was straining every nerve of his muscular young body to tear his friend loose from the grasp of the terror that held him. He could not; but a wall of black water four feet high, that came rushing down on them with an angry roar, was mightier even than the quicksand, and, seizing both the boys in its irresistible embrace, it wrenched them loose and overwhelmed them.

Chapter XXV.

SWEPT AWAY BY A FRESHET.

THE rush of waters that wrenched Binney Gibbs loose from the grasp of the quicksand which had seized him as he remained motionless for a minute, forgetful of his own danger in the excitement caused by that of the team, also flung the rope they had been holding against Glen Eddy. He held to it desperately with one hand, while, with the other arm about his companion, he prevented him from being swept away. As the mad waters dashed the boys from their feet and closed over them, it seemed as though Glen's arms must be torn from their sockets, and he would have had to let go had not Binney also succeeded in grasping the rope so that the great strain was somewhat relieved. Gasping for breath, they both rose to the surface.

A huge white object was bearing directly down on them. They could not avoid it. Glen was the first to recognize its nature. "It's the wagon!" he shouted. "Grab hold of it, and hang on for your life!"

Then it struck them and tore loose their hold of the rope. They both managed to clutch it, though Binney's slight strength was so nearly exhausted that, but for Glen, he must speedily have let go and sunk again beneath the foam-flecked waters. Now the other's sturdy frame and athletic training came splendidly to his aid. Obtaining a firm foothold in the flooded wagon, he pulled Binney up to him by the sheer strength of his muscular young arms. For a moment they stood together panting for breath, and the weaker boy clinging to the stronger.

But the water was still rising; and, as the heavily laden wagon could not float, it seemed likely to be totally submerged. "It's no use, Glen. We'll be drowned, anyhow," said Binney, despairingly.

"Oh, no, we won't. Not just yet, anyway," answered the other, trying to sustain his companion's spirits by speaking hopefully. "We can get out of the water entirely, by climbing up on top of the cover, and I guess it will bear us."

It was a suggestion worth trying; and, though the undertaking was perilous and difficult in the extreme, under the circumstances, they finally succeeded in accomplishing it, and found themselves perched on the slippery, sagging surface of the canvas cover, that, supported by stout ash bows, was stretched above the wagon.

All this time their strange craft, though not floating, was borne slowly but steadily down stream by the force of the current. Every now and then it seemed as though about to capsize; and, had it been empty, it must certainly have done so; but its heavy load, acting like ballast in a boat, kept it upright. It headed in all directions, and at times, when its wheels could revolve on the bottom of the river, it moved steadily and rapidly. It was when it got turned broadside to the current that the two shivering figures, clutching at their uncertain support, became most apprehensive, and expected it to be overturned by the great pressure brought to bear against it.

How slowly the minutes and hours dragged by! It was about midnight when the freshet struck them and they started on this most extraordinary voyage; but from that time until they saw the first streaks of rosy light in the east seemed an eternity.

More than once during the night the wagon brought up against some obstruction, and remained motionless for longer or shorter intervals of time; but it had always been forced ahead again, and made to resume its uncertain wanderings.

Now, as the welcome daylight crept slowly

"THE STRANGE CRAFT WAS BORNE SLOWLY DOWN STREAM."

over the scene, it found the strange ark, with its two occupants, again stranded, and this time immovably so. At length Glen exclaimed, joyfully: "There's the western bank, the very one we want to reach, close to us. I believe we can swim to it, as easy as not."

"But I can't swim, you know," replied Binney, dolefully.

"That's so; I forgot," said Glen, in a dismayed tone. "But look," he added, and again there was a hopeful ring to his voice, "there are the tops of some bushes between us and it. The water can't be very deep there. Perhaps we can touch bottom, and you can wade if you can't swim. I'm going over there and take soundings."

Binney dreaded being left alone, and was about to beg his companion not to desert him, but the words were checked on his lips by the thought of the reputation he had to sustain. So, as Glen pulled off his wet clothing, he said, "All right, only be very careful and don't go too far, for I think I would rather drown with you than be left here all alone."

"Never fear!" cried Glen; "swimming is about the one thing I can do. So, here goes!"

He had climbed down, and stood on the edge of the submerged wagon body as he spoke. Now he sprang far out in the yellow waters, and the next moment was making his way easily through them towards the bushes. The swift current carried him down-stream; but at length he caught one of them, and, letting his feet sink, touched bottom in water up to his neck.

"It's all right!" he shouted back to Binney. Pulling himself along from one bit of willow to another, he waded towards the bank until the water was not more than up to his waist. Then he made his way up-stream until he was some distance above the place where the wagon was stranded, and, two minutes later, he had waded and swum back to it.

Binney had watched every movement anxiously, and now he said, "That's all well enough for you; but I don't see how I am going to get there."

"By resting your hands on my shoulders and letting me swim with you till you can touch bottom, of course," answered Glen.

He could not realize Binney's dread of the water, nor what a struggle against his natural timidity took place in the boy's mind before he answered, "Very well, if you say so, Glen, I'll trust you."

While he was laying aside his water-soaked clothing and preparing for the dreaded undertaking, Glen suddenly uttered an exclamation of dismay. He had spied several horsemen riding along the river-bank towards them. Were they white men or Indians? Did their coming mean life or death?

"I'm afraid they are Indians," said Glen; "for our camp must be ten miles off."

Binney agreed with him that they must have come at least that distance during the night, and the boys watched the oncoming horsemen with heavy hearts.

"I'd rather drown than let them get me again," said Glen.

But Binney had not had the other's experience with Indians, and to him nothing could be more terrible than water.

Long and earnestly they watched, filled with alternate hopes and fears. The riders seemed to move very slowly. All at once, Glen uttered a shout of joy. "They are white men!" he cried. "I can see their hats;" and, seizing his wet shirt, he began to wave it frantically above his head.

That his signal was seen was announced by a distant cheer, and several shots fired in quick succession. A few minutes later, six white men reined in their horses on the bank, just abreast the wagon. They were hardly able to credit their eyes as they recognized, in the two naked figures clinging to it, those whom they had been so certain were long ago drowned, and for whose bodies they were searching. As they hurriedly consulted concerning how best to effect a rescue, they were amazed to see both boys clamber down from their perch, and drop into the turbid waters, one after the other. When they realized that Glen and Binney were swimming, and trying in this way to reach the shore, they forced their horses down the steep bank and dashed into the shallow overflow of the bottom-land to meet them.

At that moment Binney Gibbs, by trusting himself so implicitly to Glen's strength and skill, in an element where he was so utterly helpless, was displaying a greater courage than where, acting under impulse, he sprang from his mule the day before, and ran back to fight Indians. The bravest deeds are always those that are performed deliberately and after a careful consideration of their possible consequences.

As "Billy" Brackett, who was the first to reach the boys, relieved Glen of his burden, he exclaimed,

"Well, if I had the luck of you fellows I'd change my name to Vanderbilt and run for Congress! We were sure you were gone up this time, and the best I hoped for was to find your bodies. Instead of that, here you are, hardly out of sight of camp, perched on the top of a wagon, as chipper as a couple of sparrows after a rain-storm."

"Where is camp?" inquired Glen, who was now wading easily along beside the other's horse.

"Just around that farther bend, up there."

"What made it come so far down the river, and off the road?"

"It hasn't. It's right at the ford, where we crossed last night."

"But I thought that was at least ten miles from here."

"Ten miles! Why, my son, you must have imagined you were travelling on a four-wheeled steamboat all night, instead of an old water-logged prairie schooner. We are not, at this minute, quite a mile from the place where you started on your cruise."

It was hard for the boys to realize the truth of this statement; but so it was; and, during those tedious hours of darkness they had only travelled rods instead of miles, as they had fancied.

After the short delay necessary to recover the boys' clothing from the wagon, they were triumphantly borne back to camp by the rescuing-party. There the enthusiasm with which they were received was only equalled by the amazement of those who crowded about them and listened to the account of their adventure.

By means of a double team of mules, and some stout ropes, even the wagon on which they had made their curious voyage was recovered, and found to be still serviceable, though the greater part of its load was ruined.

The river was still an impassable stream, as wide as the Mississippi at St. Louis, and was many feet deep over the place, on its farther side, where they had camped at sunset. Thus there was no danger of another attack from Indians. Two hours after sunrise the explorers were again wending their way westward, rejoicing over their double escape, and over the recovery of the two members who had been given up as lost.

Chapter XXVI.

AFTER this day and night, crowded so full of incident, four days of steady travel brought General Lyle's expedition to a point close to the boundary - line between Kansas and Colorado, where their surveys were to begin. The last hundred miles of their journey had been through a region studded with curious masses of sandstone. These were scattered far and wide over the Plains, and rose to a height of from one hundred to three hundred feet, resembling towers, monuments, castles, and ruins of every description. It was hard to believe that many of them were not the work of human hands; and to Glen and Binney they formed an inexhaustible subject for wonder and speculation.

They were now more than three thousand feet above the sea-level; the soil became poorer with every mile; there were fewer streams, and along those that did exist timber was almost unknown.

The first line of survey was to be a hard one; for it was to run through the very worst of this country—from the Smoky Hill to the Arkansas, a region hitherto unexplored, and known only to the few buffalo hunters who had crossed it at long intervals. The distance was supposed to be about seventy miles, and there was said to be no water along the entire route. But both a transit and a level line must be run over this barren region, and the distance must be carefully measured. A good day's work for a surveying-party, engaged in running a first, or preliminary, line in an open country, is eight or ten miles; and, at this rate, the distance between the Smoky Hill and the Arkansas rivers could be covered in a week. But a week without water was out of the question, and General Lyle determined to do it in three days.

On the night before beginning this remarkable survey, every canteen and bottle that could be found was filled with water, as were several casks. Everybody drank as much as he could in the morning, and all the animals were watered the very last thing. Everything was packed and ready for a start by daylight, and long before sunrise the working-party was in the field. The first division was to run the first two miles. Its transit was set up over the last stake of the old survey that had been ended at that point, and the telescope was pointed in the direction of the course now to be taken. The division engineer, with his front flagman, had already galloped half a mile away across the plain. There they halted, and the gayly painted staff, with its fluttering red pennon, was held upright. Then it was moved to the right or left, as the transit-man, peering through his telescope, waved his right or left arm. Finally, he waved both at a time, and the front flag was thrust into the ground. It was on line.

Now the head chainman starts off on a run, with his eyes fixed on the distant flag, and dragging a hundred feet of glistening steel-links behind him. "Stick!" shouts the rear chainman, who stands beside the transit, as he grasps the end of the chain and pulls it taut. "Stuck!" answers the man in front, thrusting one of the steel pins that he carries in his hand into the ground. Then he runs on, and the rear chainman runs after him, but just a hundred feet behind.

Two axemen, one with a bundle of marked stakes in his arms, and the other carrying an axe with which to drive them, follow the chain closely. At the end of each five hundred feet they drive a stake. If stakes were not so scarce in this country, they would set one at the end of every hundred feet. It does not make much difference; for these stakes will not remain stand-

ing very long anyhow. The buffalo will soon
pull them up, by rubbing and scratching their
heads against them. At the end of every half-
mile, a mound of earth—or stones, if they can be
found—is thrown up; and these the Indians will
level whenever they come across them. Perhaps
some of them will be left, though.

While the chainmen are measuring the distance to that front flag, and the axemen are driving stakes and throwing up mounds, the transit-
man, mounted on a steady-going mule, with the
transit on his shoulder, is galloping ahead to
where the front flag awaits him. Only the back
flagman is left standing at the place from which
the first sight was taken.

The front flagman thrust a small stake in the
ground, drove a tack in its centre, and held his
flag on it before he waved the transit-man up.
Now the transit is set over this stake so that the
centre of the instrument is directly over the tack;
and while it is being made ready the front flag
is again galloping away over the rolling prairie,
far in advance of the rest of the party.

The transit-man first looks through his telescope at the back flag, now far behind him, and
waves to him to come on. Then the telescope is
reversed, and he is ready to wave the front flag
into line as soon as he stops.

The leveller, with two rodmen, all well mounted, follow behind the transit-party, noting, by means of their instruments, the elevation above sea-level of every stake that is driven.

So the work goes on with marvellous rapidity —every man and horse and mule on a run until two miles have been chained and it is time for the breathless first division to have a rest.

Mr. Hobart has watched their work carefully. He has also made some changes in his force, and is going to see what sort of a front flagman Glen Eddy will make. This is because Nettle has proved herself the fleetest pony in the whole outfit.

"Two miles in fifty-two minutes!" shouts Mr. Hobart to his men, as the stake that marks the end of ten thousand five hundred and sixty feet is driven. "Boys, we must do better than that."

"Ay, ay, sir! We will!" shout the "bald heads," as they spring to the places the first-division men are just leaving.

Mr. Hobart, Glen, and a mounted axeman are already galloping to the front. They dash across a shallow valley, lying between two great swells of the prairie, and mount the gentle slope on its farther side, a mile away. It is a long transit sight; but "Billy" Brackett can take it.

The boy who rides beside the division engineer

is very proud of his new position, and sits his
spirited mare like a young lancer. The slender,
steel-shod, red-and-white staff of his flag-pole,
bearing its gay pennon, that Glen has cut a little
longer than the others, and nicked with a swal-
low-tail, looks not unlike a lance. As the cool
morning air whistles past him, the boy's blood
tingles, his eyes sparkle, and he wonders if there
can be any more fascinating business in the world
than surveying and learning to become an engineer. He thinks of the mill and the store with
scorn. It beats them away out of sight, anyhow.

As they reach the crest of the divide, from
which they can see far away on all sides, Mr.
Hobart, using his field-glass to watch the movements of "Billy" Brackett's arms, directs Glen
where to place his flag. "Right—more—more
—away over to the right—there—steady! Left,
a little—steady—so! Drive a stake there! Now
hold your flag on it! A trifle to the right—that's
good! Drive the tack! Move him up—all right,
he's coming!" Then, leaving the axeman to point
out the stake, just driven, to the transit-man, the
engineer and his young flagman again dash forward.

"Two miles in thirty-eight minutes! That is
quick work! I congratulate you and your di-

vision, Mr. Hobart." So said the chief-engineer as the men of the second division, dripping with perspiration, completed their first run, and, turning the work over to those of the third, took their vacant places in the wagon that followed the line.

The morning sun was already glowing with heat, and by noon its perpendicular rays were scorching the arid plain with relentless fury. Men and animals alike drooped beneath it, but there was no pause in the work. It must be rushed through in spite of everything. About noon they passed a large buffalo wallow, half filled with stagnant water, that the animals drank eagerly.

That evening, when it was too dark to distinguish the cross-hairs in the instruments, the weary engineers knocked off work, with a twenty-one-mile survey to their credit. They were too tired to pitch tents that night, but spread their blankets anywhere, and fell asleep almost as soon as they had eaten supper. There was no water, no wood, and only a scanty supply of sun-dried grass. It was a dry camp.

The next day was a repetition of the first. The tired animals, suffering from both hunger and thirst, dragged the heavy wagons wearily over the long undulations of the sun-baked plain.

Occasionally they crossed dry water-courses; but at sunset they had not found a drop of the precious fluid, and another dry camp was promised for that night.

As the men of the second division drove the last stake of another twenty-one-mile run, and, leaving the line, moved slowly in the direction of camp, the mule ridden by Binney Gibbs suddenly threw up its head, sniffed the air, and, without regard to his rider's efforts to control him, started off on a run.

"Stop us! We are running away!" shouted Binney; and, without hesitation, Glen gave spurs to Nettle and dashed away in pursuit.

"What scrape are those young scatter-brains going to get into now?" growled Mr. Hobart.

"I don't know," answered "Billy" Brackett; "but whatever it is they will come out of it all right, covered with mud and glory. I suppose I might as well begin to organize the rescuing-party, though."

Chapter XXVII.

"COVERED WITH MUD AND GLORY."

As "Billy" Brackett predicted they would, the two boys did return to camp in about fifteen minutes, covered with mud and glory. At least Binney Gibbs was covered with mud, and they brought the glorious news that there were several large though shallow pools of water not more than half a mile away. Binney's mule having scented it, there was no stopping him until he had rushed to it, and, as usual, flung his rider over his head into the very middle of one of the shallow ponds. Glen had reached the place just in time to witness this catastrophe, and to roar with laughter at the comical sight presented by his companion, as the latter waded ruefully from the pond, dripping mud and water from every point.

"You take to water as naturally as a young duck, Binney!" he shouted, as soon as his laughter gave him a chance for words.

"No, indeed, I don't" sputtered poor Binney. "But somehow water always seems to take to me, and I can get nearly drowned when nobody else can find a drop to drink. As for that mule, I believe he thinks I wouldn't know how to get off his back if he didn't pitch me off."

In less than a minute after the boys got back with their report of water, half the men in camp were hastening towards it, and the entire herd of animals, in charge of a couple of teamsters, was galloping madly in the same direction. The ponds were the result of a heavy local rain of the night before; and, within a couple of days, would disappear in the sandy soil as completely as though they had never existed; but they served an admirable purpose, and the whole party was grateful to Binney Gibbs's mule for discovering them.

So refreshed were the men by their unexpected bath, and so strengthened were the animals by having plenty of water with both their evening and morning meals, that the survey of the following day covered twenty-four miles. It was the biggest day's work of transit and level on record, and could only have been accomplished under extraordinary circumstances.

This was the hardest day of the three to bear. The heat of the sun, shining from an unclouded sky, was intolerable. As far as the eye could reach there was no shadow, nor any object to break the terrible monotony of its glare. A hot wind from the south whirled the light soil aloft in suffocating clouds of dust. The men of the three divisions were becoming desperate. They knew that this killing pace could not be maintained much longer, and the twenty-four mile run was the result of a tremendous effort to reach the Arkansas River that day.

From each eminence, as they crossed it, telescope, field-glasses, and straining eyes swept the sky-line in the hope of sighting the longed-for river. Late in the afternoon some far away trees and a ribbon of light were lifted to view against the horizon by the shimmering heat waves; but this was at once pronounced to be only the tantalizing vision of the mirage.

So, in a dry camp, the exhausted men and thirsty animals passed the night. The latter, refusing to touch the parched grass or even their rations of corn, made the hours hideous with their cries, and spent their time in vain efforts to break their fastenings that they might escape and seek to quench their burning thirst.

But even this night came to an end; and, with the first eastern streaks of pink and gold so exquisitely beautiful through the rarefied atmosphere of this region, the surveyors were once more in the field. There was no merriment now, nor life in the work. It went on amid a dogged silence. The transit and level were lifted slowly, as though they were made of lead. The chain was dragged wearily along at a walk. It was evident that the limit of endurance was nearly reached. Scouts were sent out on both sides to search for water. There was no use sending anybody ahead to hunt up that mirage, or at least so thought General Lyle. His maps showed the river to be miles away; but they also showed a large creek, not far to the westward; and towards this the hopes of the party were turned. On the maps it was called "Sand Creek," a name made infamous forever by a massacre of Indians, mostly women and children, that took place on its banks in November, 1864. Then it had contained water; but now it was true to its name, and the dispirited scouts, returning from it, reported that its bed was but a level expanse of dry, glistening sand.

As this report was being made, there came a quick succession of shots from the front, and a thrill of new life instantly pervaded the whole party. What could they indicate, if not good news of some kind. The first division had completed its two miles, and the second was running the line. "Billy" Brackett was preparing for one of his famous mile sights at the front flag, with which Glen Eddy, riding beside Mr. Hobart, was wearily toiling up a distant slope. Gazing at them through his fine telescope, the transit-man could not at first understand their extraordinary actions as they reached the top. He saw Glen fling up his hat, and Mr. Hobart fire his pistol into the air. Then Glen waved his flag, while the division engineer seemed to be pointing to something in front of them.

"Well, quit your fooling and give me a sight, can't you?" growled "Billy" Brackett to himself, but directly afterwards he shouted to those near him, "I believe they've found water, and shouldn't wonder if they'd located the Arkansas itself. Then he got his "sight," waved "all right," mounted his mule, shouldered the transit, and galloped away.

He was right; they had located the Arkansas, and the alleged mirage of the evening before had been a reality after all. That night of suffering had been spent within five miles of one of the largest rivers that cross the Plains.

As Glen and Mr. Hobart reached the crest of that long slope they saw its grassy valley outspread before them. They saw the scattered timber lining its banks, and, best of all, they saw the broad, brown flood itself, rolling down to join the distant Mississippi. By shots and wav-

ings they tried to communicate the joyful in·
telligence to those who toiled so wearily behind them, and "Billy" Brackett, watching them
through his transit, had understood.

They waited on the ridge until he joined
them, and then hastened away towards the tempting river. When the next foresight was taken
Glen's flag was planted on the edge of that
famous old wagon-road of the Arkansas Valley
known to generations of Plainsmen as the Santa
Fé Trail.

Glen had hardly waved his "all right" to the
transit, before the wagons came tearing down the
slope with their mules on the keen run. The
perishing animals had seen the life-giving waters,
and it was with the greatest difficulty that they
were restrained from rushing into the river, wagons and all. The drivers only just succeeded in
casting loose the trace-chains, when each team,
with outstretched necks and husky brayings,
plunged in a body over the bank and into the
river, burying their heads up to their eyes in the
cooling flood. It seemed as though they would
drink themselves to death, and when they finally
consented to leave the river and turn their attention to the rich grasses of its bottom-lands, they
were evidently water-logged. It would be hours
before they were again fit for work.

But nobody wanted them to work. Not until the next morning would the wagons move again. The splendid runs of the last three days had earned a rest for men and animals alike. So it was granted them, and no schoolboys ever enjoyed a half-holiday more. What a luxury it was to have plenty of water again, not only to drink, but actually to wash with and bathe in! And to lie in the shade of a tree! Could anything be more delicious?

At sunrise the line was resumed; and, still working together, the three divisions ran it for fifty miles up the broad valley of the Arkansas.

A few days after striking the river they passed Bent's Fort, one of the most famous of the old Plains trading-posts built by individuals long before troops were sent out to occupy the land. Its usefulness as a trading-station had nearly departed, for already the Indians were leaving that part of the country, and those who remained were kept too busy fighting to have any time for trading. Its stout log stockade was, however, valuable to its builder as a protection against attacks from Indians led by one of his own sons. Their mother was a Cheyenne squaw, and though they, together with their only sister, had been educated in St. Louis, the same as white children, they had preferred to follow the fortunes of their mother's people on returning to the Plains. Now the Cheyennes had no more daring leader than George Bent, nor was there a girl in the tribe so beautiful as his sister. The little fort, admirably located on a high bluff overlooking the river, was filled with a curious mixture of old Plainsmen, Indians, half-breed children, ponies, mules, burros, and pet fawns. It was a place of noise and confusion at once bewildering and interesting.

At the end of fifty miles from the point at which they entered the Arkansas Valley, the explorers caught their first glimpse of the Rocky Mountains, two white clouds that they knew to be the snow-capped summits of the Spanish Peaks, a hundred miles away.

Here the expedition was divided. The first and third divisions were to cross the river and proceed southwesterly, by way of the Raton Mountains and Fort Union, to Santa Fé; while Mr. Hobart was to take the second still farther up the Arkansas Valley, and almost due west to the famous Sangre de Cristo Pass through the mountains, just north of the Spanish Peaks. For two weeks longer they worked their way slowly but steadily across the burning Plains, towards the mountains that almost seemed to recede from them as they advanced; though each day disclosed new peaks, while those already familiar loomed up higher and grander with every mile. Finally they were so near at hand that the weary toilers, choked with the alkaline dust of the Plains, and scorched with their fervent heat, could feast their eyes on the green slopes, cool, dark valleys, and tumbling cascades, rushing down from glittering snow-fields. How they longed to be among them, and with what joy did they at length leave the treeless country of which they were so tired and enter the timbered foot-hills!

Now, how deliciously cool were the nights, and how they enjoyed the roaring camp-fires. What breathless plunges they took in ice-cold streams of crystal water. How good fresh venison tasted after weeks of salt bacon and dried buffalo meat, and how eagerly they ate raw onions, and even raw potatoes, obtained at the occasional Mexican ranches found nestled here and there in the lower valleys.

"I tell you," said Glen to Binney Gibbs, who had by this time become his firm friend, "it pays to go without fresh vegetables for a couple of months, just to find out what fine things onions and potatoes are."

CHAPTER XXVIII

LOST IN A MOUNTAIN SNOW-STORM.

A WEEK was spent on the eastern slope of the mountains, running lines through the Mosca and Cuchara passes. Finally, a camp was made in a forest of balsam-firs, beside a great spring of ice-water, that bubbled from a granite basin at the summit of the Sangre de Cristo, nine thousand feet above sea-level. To Glen and Binney, who had always dwelt in a flat country, and knew nothing of mountains, this was a new and delightful experience. They never tired of gazing off on the superb panorama outspread below them. To the east, the view was so vast and boundless that it seemed as though the distant blue of the horizon must be that of the ocean itself, and that they were spanning half the breadth of a continent in a single sight. At their feet lay the Plains they had just crossed, like a great green map on which dark lines of timber and gleams of light marked the Arkansas and its tributary streams, whose waters would mingle with those of the Mississippi.

On the other hand, they could see, across the broad basin of the San Luis Valley, other ranges of unknown mountains, whose mysteries they were yet to explore. Through this western valley, flowing southward, wound the shining ribbon of the Rio Grande. Both north and south of them were mountain-peaks. To cumb to the very summit of one of these was Glen's present ambition, and his longing eyes were turned more often to the snow-capped dome that rose in solemn majesty on the south side of the pass than in any other direction. He even succeeded in persuading Binney Gibbs that to climb that mountain would be just a little better fun than anything else that could be suggested. Still, he did not see any prospect of their being allowed to make the attempt, and so tried not to think of it.

On the first evening, after camp had been pitched on the summit of the pass, he sat on a chunk of moss-covered granite, gazing meditatively into the glowing coals of a glorious fire. He imagined he had succeeded in banishing all thoughts of that desirable mountain-top from his mind, and yet, all of a sudden, he became aware that it was the very thing he was thinking of. He gave himself a petulant shake as he realized this, and was about to move away, when " Billy "

Brackett, who sat on the end of a log near him, spoke up and said,

"Glen, how would you like to try a bit of mountain climbing with me to-morrow?"

"I'd like it better than anything I know of," answered the boy, eagerly.

"All right, it's a go, then; you see the chief is going off on an exploration with the topographer; and, as we can't run any lines till he comes back, he asked me if I'd take a couple of fellows and measure the height of that peak."

"Do you mean to chain from here away up there?" asked Glen, in astonishment, glancing dubiously up at the dim form towering above them.

"Chain! Not much, I don't!" laughed Brackett. "I mean carry up a barometer, and measure with it."

"How?" asked Glen, to whom this was a novel idea.

"Easy enough. We know that, roughly speaking, a barometer varies a little less than one tenth of an inch with every hundred feet of elevation. For instance, if it reads 21.22 where we now are, it will read 21.14 a hundred feet higher, or 20.40 at an elevation of a thousand feet above this. There are carefully prepared tables showing the exact figures."

"Can't you do it by boiling water, too?" asked Binney Gibbs, who had approached them unobserved, and was an interested listener of this explanation.

"Certainly you can," answered "Billy" Brackett, looking up with some surprise at the young scholar. "By boiling water we have a neat check on the barometer; for, on account of the rarefication of the air, water boils at one degree less of temperature for about every five hundred feet of elevation."

"Then what is the use of levelling?" asked Glen.

"Because these figures are only approximate, and cannot be relied upon for nice work. But where did you learn about such things, Grip?"

"At the Brimfield High School," answered Binney with some confusion; for he was not really so boastful of his scholarship as he had once been.

"Well, how would you like to join our climbing-party? I'm going to take Glen along for his muscle, and I'll take you for your brains if you want to go."

"I think I'd like to try it, though perhaps I won't be able to get to the very top," answered Binney.

The modesty that this boy had learned from his rough Plains experience would have surprised his Brimfield acquaintances could they have seen it.

"Very well, then, we will start at sunrise in the morning. We'll each carry a hatchet, a knife, matches in water-tight cases, and a good bit of lunch. I'll carry the barometer, Glen shall take charge of the thermometer, and 'Grip' shall bring along his brains. Now I'd advise you both to turn in, and lay up a supply of rest sufficient to carry you through a harder day's work than any we've done on this trip yet."

The sun was just lifting his red face above the distant rim of the Plains, and its scant beams were bathing the snow-capped peak in a wonderful rosy glow, as the three mountain climbers left camp the next morning. Each one bore the light weight allotted to him, and, in addition, Glen carried a raw-hide lariat hung over his shoulders.

Having noted the compass bearings of their general course, they plunged directly into the dense fir forest with which this flank of the mountain was covered to a height of a thousand feet or so above them. For several hours they struggled through it, sometimes clambering over long lanes of fallen trees, prostrated by fierce wind-storms, and piled in chaotic heaps so thickly that often, for half a mile at a time, their feet did not touch the ground. Then they came to a region of enormous granite blocks, ten to thirty feet high, over many of which they were obliged to make their way as best they could. Now they began to find patches of snow, and the timber only appeared in scattered clumps.

From here their course led up through an enormous gorge, or cleft, that grew narrower as they ascended, until it terminated in a long, steep slope of boulders and loose rocks. Here they encountered the first real danger of the ascent. Every now and then a boulder, that appeared firmly seated until burdened with the weight of one of them, would give way and go crashing and thundering down with great leaps behind them until lost in the forest below.

It was noon when they emerged on a narrow, shelf-like plateau above the gorge. Here stood the last clump of stunted trees. Above them stretched the glistening snow-fields, pierced by crags of splintered granite. Rock, ice, and snow to the very summit. Here Binney said he could go no farther; and here, after building a fire and eating their lunch, the others left him to await their return.

A sheer wall of smooth, seamless rock, hundreds of feet in height, bounded one side of the shelf, and a precipice, almost as sheer, the other.

For half a mile or so did Glen and his companion follow it, seeking some place at which they might continue their ascent. Finally it narrowed almost to a point, that terminated in an immense field of snow sloping down, smooth and spotless, for a thousand feet below them, to a tiny blue-black lake. Beyond the snow-field the ascent seemed possible; and, by cutting footholes in it with their hatchets, they managed to cross it in safety.

For two hours longer they struggled upward; and then, within a few hundred feet of the summit, they could get no farther. In vain did they try every point that offered the faintest hope of success, and at last were forced to give it up. They noted the reading of the barometer, and with a few shavings and slivers cut from its outside case they made a tiny blaze, and, as Glen expressed it, boiled a thermometer in a tin cup.

They were now as impatient to descend as they had been to climb upward, and even more so; for the brightness of the day had departed, and ominous clouds were gathering about them. The air was bitterly cold; and, with their few minutes' cessation from violent exercise, they were chilled to the bone. So they hastened to retrace their rugged way, sliding, leaping, hanging by their hands, and dropping from ledge to ledge.

taking frightful risks in their eagerness to escape the threatened storm, or at any rate to meet it in some more sheltered spot. If they could only reach the shelf-like ledge, at the farther end of which Binney Gibbs awaited them, they would feel safe. They had nearly done so, but not quite, when the storm burst upon them in a fierce, blinding, whirling rush of snow, that took away their breath and stung like needles. It seemed to penetrate their clothing. It bewildered them. It was so dense that they could not see a yard ahead of them. They had already started to cross that long, sloping snow-field, beyond which lay the rocky shelf. To go back would be as dangerous as to proceed. They could not stay where they were. The deadly chill of the air would speedily render them incapable of maintaining their foothold.

The assistant engineer was leading the way, with his companion a full rod behind him. The former dared not turn his head; but he shouted encouragingly that they were almost across, and with a few more steps would reach a place of safety.

Then came a swirling, shrieking blast, before which he bowed his head. He thought he heard a cry; but could not tell. It might only have been the howl of the fierce wind. He reached the shelf of rock in safety, and turned to look for his companion; but Glen was not to be seen.

Blinded by that furious blast, the boy had missed his footing. The next instant he was sliding, helplessly, and with frightful velocity, down that smooth slope of unyielding snow, towards the blue lake hidden in the storm-cloud far beneath him.

Chapter XXIX.

PLUNGING INTO A LAKE OF ICE-WATER.

As "Billy" Brackett turned and missed the companion whom he supposed was close behind him, his heart sank like lead. In vain did he shout. Not even an echo answered him. His loudest tones were snatched from his lips by the wind, torn into fragments, and indistinguishably mingled with its mocking laughter. It was barely possible that Glen might have turned back; and, with the slender hope thus offered, the engineer retraced his perilous way across the snow-field to the place where they last stood together. It was empty and awful in its storm-swept loneliness. A great terror seized hold upon the man's stout heart; and, as he again crossed the treacherous snow, he trembled so that his reaching the rocky shelf beyond was little short of a miracle.

Then he hastened to the place where Binney Gibbs anxiously awaited the return of his friends. He had kept up a roaring fire, knowing that it would be a welcome sight to them, especially since the setting-in of the storm. Its coming had filled him with anxiety and uneasy forebodings, so that he hailed "Billy" Brackett's appearance with a glad shout of welcome. It died on his lips as he noted the expression on the engineer's face; and, with a tremble of fear in his voice, he asked, "Where is Glen?"

"I don't know," was the answer.

"Do you mean that he is lost on the mountain in this storm?" cried Binney, aghast at the terrible possibilities thus suggested.

"Not only that, but I have not the faintest hope that he will ever be found again," replied the other; and then he told all he knew of what had happened.

Although, for their own safety, they should already be hurrying towards camp, Binney insisted on going to the place where his friend had last been seen. The snow-squall had passed when they reached it, but the clouds still hung thick about them; and Binney shuddered as he saw the smooth white slide that vanished in the impenetrable mist but a few rods below them. In vain they shouted. In vain they fired every shot contained in the only pistol they had brought with them. There was no answer. And, finally, without a hope that they would ever see Glen Eddy again, they sadly retraced their steps and reached camp just as the complete darkness, that would have rendered their farther progress impossible, shut in.

No one was more loved in that camp than Glen, and no loss from the party could have been more keenly felt. It was with heavy hearts that they sought their blankets that night; and, the next evening, when the search-party, that had been out all day without finding the faintest trace of the missing boy, returned, they talked of him in low tones as of one who had gone from them forever.

The following morning the camp in the pass was broken, and two days later a line had been run down the western slope of the mountains, to the edge of the San Luis Valley, near Fort Garland—one of the most charmingly located military posts of the West.

In the meantime Glen Eddy was not only alive and well, but, at the very minute his companions were approaching Fort Garland he was actually assisting to prepare the quarters of its commandant for a wedding that was to take place in them that evening.

For a moment, after he missed his foothold on the upper edge of the treacherous snow-field, and began to shoot down the smooth surface of its long slope, he imagined that he was about to be dashed in pieces, and resigned all hope of escape from the fearful peril that had so suddenly overtaken him. Then the thought of the blue-black lake, with its walls of purple and red-stained granite, that he had seen lying at the foot of this very slope, flashed into his mind. A thrill shot through him as he thought of the icy plunge he was about to take. Still, that was better than to be hurled over a precipice. The boy had even sufficient presence of mind to hold his feet close together, and attempt to guide himself so that they should strike the water first.

He might have glided down that slope for seconds, or minutes, or even hours, for all that he knew of the passage of time. He seemed to be moving with great speed, and yet, in breathless anticipation of the inevitable plunge that, in fancy, he felt himself to be taking with each instant, his downward flight seemed indefinitely prolonged.

At length the suspense was ended. Almost with the quickness of thought the boy passed into a region of dazzling sunlight, was launched into space, and found himself sinking down, down, down, as though he would never stop, in water so cold that its chill pierced him like knives, and compressed his head as with a band of iron.

Looking up through the crystal sheet, he could see an apparently endless line of bubbles rising from where he was to the surface, and, after a while, he began to follow them. With a breathless gasp he again reached the blessed air, and, dashing the water from his eyes, began to consider his situation. He was dazed and bewildered at finding himself still alive and apparently none the worse for his tremendous slide. Although he was in bright sunlight, the mountain-side down which he had come was hidden beneath dense folds of cloud, out of which he seemed to have dropped.

Gently paddling with his hands, just enough to keep himself afloat, Glen looked anxiously about for some beach or other place at which he might effect a landing, but could discover none. The upper edge of the snow-field, that bounded the lake on one side, projected far over the water, so that, while he might swim under it, there was no possibility of getting on it. On all other sides sheer walls of rock rose from the water, without a trace of beach, or even of boulders, at their base.

In all this solid wall there was but one break. Not far from where Glen swam, and just beyond the snow-field, a narrow cleft appeared ; and from it came an indistinct roar of waters. Glen felt himself growing numbed and powerless. He must either give up at once, and tamely allow himself to sink where he was, or he must swim to that cleft, and take his chances of getting out through it. He fully expected to find a waterfall just beyond the gloomy portal, and he clearly realized what his fate would be if it were there. But whatever he did must be done quickly. He knew that, and began to swim towards the cleft.

As he approached it, he felt himself impelled onward by a gentle current that grew stronger with each moment. Now he could not go back if he would. He passed between two lofty walls of rock, and, instead of dashing over a waterfall, was borne along by a swift, smooth torrent that looked black as ink in the gloom of its mysterious channel.

Ere the swimmer had traversed more than fifty yards of this dim waterway, the channel turned sharply to the left, and the character of the lower portion of its wall, on that side, changed from a precipice to a slope. In another moment Glen's feet touched bottom, and he was slowly dragging his numbed and exhausted body ashore.

Although the sun was still shining on the mountain-side, far above him, it was already twilight where he was, and he had no desire to explore that stream farther in darkness. It would be bad enough by daylight. In fact, he was so thankful to escape from that icy water that, had the light been increasing instead of waning at that moment, he would probably have lingered long on those blessed rocks before tempting it further.

Now, as he gazed about him in search of some place in which, or on which, to pass the long hours of darkness, his eye fell on a confused pile of driftwood not far away. Here was a prize indeed. He had matches, and, thanks to "Billy" Brackett, they were still dry. Now he could have a fire. He found the driftwood to be a mass of branches and tree-trunks, bleached to the whiteness of bones, and evidently brought down by some much higher water than the present. They were lodged in the mouth of a deep water-worn hollow in the rock, and converted a certain portion of it into a sort of a cave. Creeping in behind this wooden wall of gnarled roots, twisted branches, and splintered trunks, the shivering boy felt for his hatchet; but it had disappeared. His knife still remained in its sheath, however, and with it he finally managed, though with great difficulty on account of the numbness of his hands, to cut off a little pile of slivers and shavings from a bit of pine.

In another moment the cave was illumined

with a bright glow from one of his precious matches, and a tiny flame was creeping up through the handful of kindling. With careful nursing and judicious feeding the little flame rapidly increased in strength and brightness, until it was lighting the whole place with its cheerful glow, and was leaping, with many cracklings, through the entire mass of driftwood.

Before starting that fire, it seemed to Glen that no amount of heat could be unwelcome, or that he could ever be even comfortably warm again. He discovered his mistake, however, when he was finally forced to abandon his cave entirely, and seek refuge in the open air from the intense heat with which it was filled. Not until his pile of wood had burned down to a bed of glowing coals could he return.

His couch that night was certainly a hard one, but it was as warm and dry as a boy could wish. If he only had something to eat! But he had not; so he went to sleep instead, and slept soundly until daylight—which meant about an hour after sunrise in the world beyond that narrow cañon.

If he was hungry the night before, how ravenous he was in the morning. He even cut off a bit of the rawhide lariat which he still retained, and tried to chew it. It was so very unsatisfactory a morsel that it helped him to realize the necessity of speedily getting out of that place and hunting for some food more nourishing than lariats.

Chapter XXX.

DOWN THE LONELY CAÑON.

Glen had been conscious, ever since reaching his haven, of a dull, distant roar coming up from the cañon below him; and now, after an hour of scrambling, climbing, slipping, but still managing to keep out of the water, he discovered the fall that he had anticipated, and found himself on its brink. It was a direct plunge of a hundred feet, and the body of water very nearly occupied the whole of a narrow chasm between two cliffs similar to those at the outlet of the lake. A few feet of the rocky dam, where Glen stood, were bare of water; but its face fell away as steep and smooth as that over which the stream took its plunge. Only, in the angle formed by it and the side of the cañon, a mass of débris had collected that reached about half-way up to where Glen stood, or to within fifty feet of the brink. On it grew a few stunted trees, the first vegetation he had seen since taking his slide. Below that place the way seemed more open, and as though it might be possible to traverse.

But how should he get down? He dared not leap; he could not fly. But he still had the lariat. It was forty feet long. If he could only fasten it where he stood, he might slide down its length and then drop.

Vainly he searched for some projecting point of rock about which to make his rope fast. There was none. All was smooth and water-worn. There was a crack. If he only had a stout bit of wood to thrust into it he might fasten the lariat to that. But he had not seen the smallest stick since leaving his sleeping-place. Some unburned branches were still left there; but the idea of going back over that perilous road, through the gloom of the cañon, was most unpleasant to contemplate. He hated to consider it. Still, before long it would be much more unpleasant to remain where he was, for he was already realizing the first pangs of starvation.

So he wearily retraced his steps, procured a stout branch, and, after two hours of the most arduous toil, again stood on the brink of the waterfall. Forcing the stick as far as possible into the crack, and wedging it firmly with bits of rock, he attached the raw-hide rope to it, and flung the loose end over the precipice. Then, hanging over the edge, he grasped the rope firmly and slowly slid down. As he reached the end he hesitated for a moment, and glanced below. His feet dangled on a level with the top of the upmost tree. He dreaded to drop, but there was nothing else to do, and the next moment he was rolling and scrambling in the loose gravel and rounded pebbles of the heap of débris. At last he brought up against a tree-trunk, bruised and shaken, but with unbroken bones.

He had now overcome the most difficult part of his hazardous trip; and, though the way was still so rough as to demand the exercise of the utmost care and skill and the use of every ounce of strength he possessed, it presented no obstacles that these could not surmount.

Finally, some time in the afternoon, he came to a narrow strip of meadow-land, where flowers were blooming amid the grass, and on which warm sunlight was streaming. Here, too, he found a few blueberries, which he ate ravenously. What should he do for something more substantial? He was close beside the stream, which here flowed quietly, with pleasant ripplings, when he was startled by a splash in it. It must have been a fish jumping. Why had he not thought of fish before? How should he catch them?

Necessity is the best sharpener of wits, and, in less than half an hour, Glen was fishing with a

line made of fibres from the inner skin of spruce
bark, a hook formed of a bent pin, baited with a
grasshopper, and the whole attached to a crooked
bit of branch.   Not only was he fishing, but he
was catching the most beautiful brook-trout he
had ever seen almost as fast as he could re-bait
and cast his rude tackle.   There was no art required.   Nobody had ever fished in these waters
before, and the trout were apparently as eager
to be caught as he was to catch them.

Glen had not neglected to light a fire before
he began his fishing, and by the time half a dozen
of the dainty little fellows were caught a fine bed
of hot coals was awaiting them.   The boy knew
very little of the art of cooking, but what he did
know was ample for the occasion.   His fish were
speedily cleaned, laid on the coals for a minute,
turned, left a minute longer, and eaten.   When
the first half-dozen had disappeared he caught
more, and treated them in the same way.   He had
no salt, no condiments, no accessories of any kind,
save the sauce of a hunger closely allied to starvation; but that supplied everything.   It rendered that feast of half-cooked brook-trout the
most satisfactory meal he had ever eaten.

When, at last, his hunger was entirely appeased,
the sun had set, and another night without shelter or human companionship was before him;

but what did he care? As he lay in front of his fire, on an elastic, sweet-scented bed of small spruce boughs, with a semicircle of larger ones planted in the ground behind him, and their feathery tips drooping gracefully above his head, he was as happy and well-content as ever in his life. He had conquered the wilderness, escaped from one of its most cunningly contrived prison-houses, and won from it the means of satisfying his immediate wants. He enjoyed a glorious feeling of triumph and independence. To be sure, he had no idea of where he was, nor where the stream would lead him; but he had no intention of deserting it. He realized that his safest plan was to follow it. Eventually it must lead him to the Rio Grande, and there he would surely be able to rejoin his party, if he did not find them sooner.

He was in no hurry to leave the pleasant strip of flower-strewn meadow the next morning, nor did he, until he had caught and eaten a hearty breakfast, and laid in a supply of trout for at least one more meal.

The third night found him still on the bank of his stream, which was flowing happily, with many a laugh and gurgle, through a narrow but wonderfully beautiful valley, carpeted with a luxuriant growth of grass and dotted with clumps of cedars. For this night's camp he constructed a rude hut of slender poles and branches, similar to the Indian wick-i-ups he had seen on the Plains. In it he slept on a bed high heaped with soft grasses and cedar twigs that was a perfect cradle of luxury.

As Glen emerged from his hut at sunrise he was almost as startled at seeing a herd of several black-tailed (mule) deer, feeding within a hundred feet of him, as they were to see him. Pausing for a good stare at him, for the black-tailed deer is among the most inquisitive animals in the world, they bounded away with tremendous leaps, and disappeared behind a cedar thicket. A minute later Glen was again startled; this time by the report of a rifle from some distance down the valley. He had just been wishing for his own rifle, the sight of deer having suggested that venison would be a very pleasant change from a steady fish diet, and now he hurried away in the direction of the shot.

He walked nearly half a mile before coming so suddenly upon the hunter who had fired that shot, and was now engaged in dressing one of those very black-tailed deer, that the latter discovered him at the same moment, and paused in his work to examine the new-comer keenly. He was a man past middle age, squarely built, of medium height, and, as he stood up, Glen saw that he was somewhat bow-legged. His hair was thin and light in color, and his face was beardless. It was seamed and weather-beaten, the cheek-bones were high and prominent, and the keen eyes were gray. He was dressed in a complete hunting-suit of buckskin, and the rifle, lying beside him, was of an old-fashioned, long-barrelled, muzzle - loading pattern. He looked every inch, what he really was, a typical Plainsman of the best kind, possessed of an honest, kindly nature, brave and just, a man to be feared by an enemy and loved by a friend. He gazed earnestly at Glen as the latter walked up to him, though neither by look nor by word did he betray any curiosity.

"I don't know who you are, sir," said the boy, "but I know I was never more glad to see anybody in my life, for I've been wandering alone in these mountains for three days."

"Lost?" asked the other, laconically.

"Well, not exactly lost," replied Glen. Then, as clearly and briefly as possible, he related his story, which the other followed with close attention and evident interest.

"You did have a close call, and you've had a blind trail to follow since, for a fact. It sorter looks as though you'd showed sand, and I shouldn't wonder if you was the right stuff to make a man of," said the hunter, approvingly, when the recital was ended. "How old are you?"

"I think I am about sixteen," answered the boy.

"Just the age I was when I first crossed the Mississip and struck for this country, where I've been ever since. What are you going to do now?"

"I'm going to ask you to give me a slice of that venison for my breakfast, and then tell me the best way to rejoin my party," answered Glen.

"Of course I'll give you all the deer-meat you can eat, and we'll have it broiling inside of five minutes. Then, if you'll come along with me to the fort, I reckon we'll find your outfit there; or, if they ain't, the commandant will see to it that you do find them. You know him, don't you?"

"No, I don't even know who he is. What is his name?"

This question seemed, for some reason, to amuse the hunter greatly, and he laughed silently for a moment before replying: "His name is, rightly, 'Colonel Carson,' and since he's got command of a fort they've given him the title of 'General Carson;' but all the old Plainsmen and mountainmen that's travelled with him since he was your age call him 'Kit Carson,' or just 'Old Kit.' Perhaps you've heard tell of him?"

Indeed, Glen had heard of the most famous scout the Western Plains ever produced; and, with the prospect of actually seeing and speaking to him, he felt amply repaid for his recent trials and sufferings.

Chapter XXXI.

KIT CARSON'S GOLD MINE.

WHILE the hunter was talking to Glen, he was also preparing some slices of venison for broiling, and lighting a small fire. Anxious to be of use, as well as to have breakfast as soon as possible, the boy set about collecting wood for the fire. This, by the hunter's advice, he broke and split into small pieces, that it might the sooner be reduced to coals; and, while he was doing this, he told his new friend of his experience in cooking trout.

"I reckon that was better than eating them raw," said the latter, with an amused smile, "but if we had some now, I think I could show you a better way than that to cook them, though we haven't got any fry-pan."

"Perhaps I can catch some," suggested Glen, pulling his rude fishing-tackle from his pocket, as he looked about for some sort of a pole. "And I think I could do it quicker if you would lend me your hat for a few minutes. You see mine got lost while I was coasting down that mountain-side, or in the lake, I don't know which," he added, apologetically.

Here the hunter actually laughed aloud. "You don't expect to catch trout with a hat, do you?" he asked.

"Oh, no, indeed. I only want it to catch grasshoppers with. It's such slow work catching them, one at a time, with your hands; but, with a hat as big as yours, I could get a great many very quickly," and the boy gazed admiringly at the broad-brimmed sombrero worn by the other.

The stranger willingly loaned his hat to Glen, who seemed to amuse him greatly, and the latter soon had, not only all the grasshoppers he wanted, but a fine string of fish as well. By this time the fire had produced a bed of coals, and the slices of venison, spitted on slender sticks thrust into the ground, so as to be held just above them, were sending forth most appetizing odors.

Obeying instructions, Glen cleaned his fish, and gathered a quantity of grass, which he wet in the stream. The hunter had scooped out a shallow trench in the earth beside the fire, and had filled it with live coals. Above these he now spread a layer of damp grass, on which he laid the fish, covering them in turn with another layer of grass. Over this he raked a quantity of red-hot embers, and then covered the whole with a few handfuls of earth.

Ten minutes later the trout were found to be thoroughly cooked, and Glen was both thinking and saying that no fish had ever tasted so good. After eating this most satisfactory breakfast, and having hung the carcase of the deer to a branch where it would be beyond the reach of wolves until it could be sent for, Glen and his new companion started down the valley. As they walked, the latter explained to the boy that, many years before, while trapping on that very stream, he had discovered gold in its sands. Recently he had employed a number of Mexicans to work for him, and had started some placer diggings about a mile below where they then were.

This interested Glen greatly; for all of his dreams had been of discovering gold somewhere in this wonderful Western country, and he was most desirous of learning something of the process of procuring it. As they talked, they came in sight of several tents and brush huts, standing near the inner end of a long sand-bar, that extended diagonally nearly across the stream. A rude dam built along its upper side had diverted the water from it, so that a large area of sand and gravel was left dry. On this a dozen men were at work, digging with shovel and pick, or rocking cradles. Glen had heard of miners' cradles, or "rockers," but he had never seen one. Now he laughed at the resemblance between them and the low wooden cradles babies were rocked in.

They were rough boxes mounted on rockers, of which the one at the forward end was a little lower than the other, so as to give the cradle a slight slope in that direction. Each had an iron grating placed across its upper end, and a few wooden cleats nailed crosswise of its bottom. A hole was cut in its foot-board, and a handle, by means of which it was rocked, was fastened to its head-board. There were two men to each cradle: one to shovel dirt on to its grating, and the other to rock it and pour water over this dirt to wash it through. The grating was so fine that only the smallest pebbles could pass through it. As the dirt and water fell to the bottom of the cradle, and ran through it to the opening in the foot-board, the fine particles of gold sank, of their own weight, and lodged against the cleats. From these it was carefully gathered several times each day by the white overseer who had charge of the diggings, and sent to Fort Garland for safe-keeping.

Glen's guide also showed him how to wash out

a panful of gold - bearing earth, as prospectors do. He picked up a shallow iron pan, filled it with earth, and, holding it half immersed in the stream with its outer edge inclined from him, shook it rapidly to and fro, with a semi-rotary motion. In a minute all the earth had been washed out, and only a deposit of black sand, containing a number of yellow particles, was left on the bottom. The hunter said this black sand was iron, and could be blown away from about the gold after it was dry, or drawn away with a magnet.

The boy was greatly pleased to be allowed to attempt this operation for himself, and felt quite like a successful miner when told that the gold yielded by his first panful was worth about thirty cents.

While he was thus engaged a swarthy-complexioned soldier, evidently a Mexican, though he wore a United States uniform, came riding up the valley, raised his hand in salute to the hunter, and exchanged a few words with him. The latter hesitated for a moment, and then, after speaking again to the soldier, who immediately dismounted, he said to Glen, "I find that I must return to the fort at once. So if you will take this man's horse, and ride with me, I shall be glad of your company." His own horse was standing near by, and in another minute they were riding rapidly down the little valley, with the mining camp already out of sight.

After a mile or so the stream that Glen had followed for so long led them into the broad expanse of the San Luis Valley, up which they turned, and speedily came in sight of the low white walls of Fort Garland, surrounding a tall staff from which an American flag floated lazily in the warm, sun-lit air.

Although Glen did not know much about soldiers, or the meaning of military forms, he was somewhat surprised to see the guard at the main entrance of the fort turn hurriedly out and present arms as they clattered in past them. He quickly forgot this incident though, in his admiration of the interior, now opened before him. It was a large square, enclosed on all sides by low comfortable-looking buildings of adobe, neatly whitewashed, and in some cases provided with green blinds and wide piazzas. A hard, smooth driveway ran in front of them, and the middle of the enclosure was occupied by a well-turfed parade-ground, at one end of which stood a battery of light field-pieces. The chief beauty of the place lay in a little canal of crystal water, that ran entirely around the parade-ground. It was as cool and sparkling as that of its parent mountain stream, flowing just beyond the fort, and the refreshing sound of its rippling pervaded the whole place.

Riding to the opposite side of the enclosure, the hunter and his companion dismounted in front of one of the houses with blinds and a piazza. This the former invited Glen to enter, and at the same moment an orderly stepped up and took their horses. In a cool, dimly lighted room, Glen's new friend asked him to be seated and wait a few moments. In about fifteen minutes the orderly who had taken the horses entered the room, and saying to Glen that General Carson would like to see him, ushered him into an adjoining apartment. For a moment the boy did not recognize the figure, clad in a colonel's uniform, that was seated beside a writing-table. But, as the latter said, "Well, sir, I was told that you wished to see the commandant," he at once knew the voice for that of his friend the hunter, and, with a tone of glad surprise, he exclaimed,

"Why, sir, are you—"

"Yes," replied the other, laughing, "I am old Kit Carson, at your service, and I bid you a hearty welcome to Fort Garland."

Then he told Glen that one of his daughters was to be married that evening to an officer of the post. They had been engaged for some time, but there had been nobody to marry them until that day, when a priest from Taos had stopped at the fort on his way to the upper Rio Grande settlements. As he must continue his journey the next morning, the colonel had been sent for, and it was decided that the wedding should come off at once.

Thus it happened that Glen was assisting to decorate the commandant's quarters with flags and evergreens when Mr. Hobart and " Billy " Brackett, who had come on a little in advance of the rest of the party, rode up to pay their respects to Colonel Carson. He went out to meet them, and, being fond of giving pleasant surprises, did not say a word concerning Glen; but, after an exchange of greetings, led them directly into the room where he was at work. The boy was standing on a box fastening a flag to the wall above his head, as the men entered. The light from a window fell full upon him, and they recognized him at once.

Chapter XXXII.

A NEW MEXICAN WEDDING.

For a moment the amazement of the two men at again beholding the lad whom they were fully persuaded was dead would neither allow them to speak nor move. Then "Billy" Brackett walked softly over to where Glen was standing, and gave one of his legs a sharp pinch.

The startled boy, who had not noticed his approach, leaped to the floor with a cry of mingled pain and surprise.

"I only wanted to be sure you were real, old man, and not a ghost," said "Billy" Brackett, trying to speak in his usual careless tone; but the tears that stood in the honest fellow's eyes, as he wrung the boy's hand, showed how deeply he was affected, and how truly he had mourned the loss of his young friend.

Nor was Mr. Hobart less moved, and, as he grasped Glen's hand, he said, "My dear boy, I honestly believe this is the happiest moment of my life."

They did not stop to ask for his story then·

but insisted on taking him at once out to the camp that was being pitched just beyond the fort, that the rest of the party might share their joy as speedily as possible.

The boys were so busily engaged with their evening duties that the little party was not noticed until they were close at hand. Then somebody, gazing sharply at the middle figure of the three who approached, cried out, "If that isn't Glen Matherson, it's his twin brother!"

Everybody paused in what he was doing, and every eye was turned in the same direction. For a moment there was a profound silence. Then came a great shout of joyful amazement. Everything was dropped; and, with one accord, the entire party made a rush for the boy whom they all loved, and whom they had never expected to see again.

How they yelled, and cheered, and failed to find expressions for their extravagant delight! As for Binney Gibbs, he fairly sobbed as he held Glen's hand, and gazed into the face of this comrade for whom he had mourned, and whom he once thought he hated.

Although, at first sight, it seems almost incredible that so many adventures should happen to one boy on a single trip, it must be remembered that, with the exception of Binney, Glen was the youngest of the party, and consequently more likely to be reckless and careless than any of the others. He was also one of those persons who, while everybody around them is moving along quietly and soberly, are always getting into scrapes, and coming out of each one bright, smiling, and ready for another. Then, too, he was a stout, fearless fellow, with perfect confidence in himself that led him into, and out of, situations from which such boys as Binney Gibbs would steer clear.

An amusing feature of Glen's adventures was, that while his companions were ready to sympathize with him on account of his sufferings and hardships, it never seemed to occur to him that he had had anything but a good time, and one to be remembered with pleasure. Thus, in the present instance, according to his own account, his slide down the mountain-side had been the jolliest coast he ever took. His swim in the lake had been cold, but then it had not lasted long, and he had enjoyed the fire and the warmth of the cave all the more for it. As for his subsequent experiences, he related them in such a way that, before he finished, his listeners began to regard him as one of the most fortunate and to-be-envied fellows of their acquaintance. They seemed to be crossing the Plains and mountains

In the most prosaic manner, without doing anything in particular except work, while, to this boy, the trip was full of adventures and delightful experiences. Would these incidents seem so pleasant to him if he were as old as they? Perhaps not.

They were all to enjoy one novel experience that very evening, though; for Glen brought an invitation from Colonel Carson for them to attend the wedding, and of course they promptly accepted it. As it was to be an early affair, they hurried to the fort as soon as supper was over, and found the guests already assembling in a large room, from which every article of furniture had been removed. It was a motley gathering, in which were seen the gay uniforms of soldiers, the buckskin of trappers, the gaudy serapes of Mexican Cabelleros, the flannel shirts and big boots of the engineers, and the blanketed forms of stolid-faced Ute Indians, for whom Kit Carson was acting as agent at that time.

The company was ranged about three sides of the room, close against the walls; and, when they were thus disposed, a door on the vacant side opened, and a Mexican woman, bearing a large basket of candles, entered. Giving a candle to each guest, and lighting it for him, she indicated by signs that he was to hold it above his head. So the guests became living candle-sticks, and, when all their candles were lighted, the illumination was quite brilliant enough even for a wedding.

Everything being ready, the door through which the candles had been brought again opened, and the bridal party entered. First came the priest, then Kit Carson and his wife, who was a Mexican woman from Taos. Behind them walked the couple who were to be married. The bride was a slender, olive-complexioned girl, dressed very simply in white, while the groom wore the handsome uniform of a lieutenant of cavalry. The rear of the procession was brought up by a bevy of black-haired and black-eyed señoritas, sisters and cousins of the bride.

The priest read the wedding service in Latin, and the bride made her responses in Spanish, so that the few English words spoken by the groom were all that most of the spectators understood. As "Billy" Brackett afterwards remarked, it was evidently necessary to be liberally educated to get married in that country.

At the conclusion of the ceremony the entire wedding-party, with the exception of the bride's father, disappeared, and were seen no more; while Colonel Carson led his guests into a neighboring room, where the wedding supper was served.

18

Here the famous scout, surrounded by the tried comrades of many a wild campaign, entertained the company by calling on these for one anecdote after another of the adventures that had been crowded so thickly into their lives. This was a rare treat to the new-comers, especially to Glen Eddy and Binney Gibbs, to whom the thrilling tales, told by the boy trappers, scouts, hunters, and soldiers who had participated in them, were so real and vivid that, before this delightful evening was over, it seemed as though they too must have taken part in the scenes described.

In spite of the late hours kept by most of the engineers that night, their camp was broken by daylight, and at sunrise they were off on the line as usual, for September was now well advanced, and there were mountain ranges yet to be crossed that would be impassable after winter had once fairly set in. So, leaving the pleasant army post and their hospitable entertainers in it, they picked up their line, and, running it out over the broad San Luis Valley to the Rio Grande, began to follow that river into the very heart of New Mexico.

Glen was more than glad to find himself once more on Nettle's back, and again bearing the front flag in advance of the party. He was also surprised to find what a barren place the valley that had looked so beautiful and desirable from the mountains really was. Its sandy soil only supported a thick growth of sage brush, that yielded a strong aromatic fragrance when bruised or broken, and which rendered the running of the line peculiarly toilsome. It was a relief to reach the great river of New Mexico, and find themselves in the more fertile country immediately bordering on it. Here, too, they found numbers of quaint Mexican towns, of which they passed one or more nearly every day.

These were full of interest to the young explorers. While looking at their low flat-roofed houses, built of adobe, or great sun-dried bricks of mud and straw, it was hard to realize that they were still in America and traversing one of the territories of the United States. All their surroundings were those of the far East, and the descriptions in the Bible of life and scenes in Palestine applied perfectly to the valley of the Rio Grande as they saw it. The people were dark-skinned, with straight, black hair; and while the young children ran about nearly naked, their elders wore loose, flowing garments, and, if not barefooted, were shod with sandals of raw hide or plaited straw.

The square houses, with thick walls, broken only by occasional narrow unglazed windows, were exactly like those of the Biblical pictures.

Inside, the floors were of hard-beaten clay, and there were neither tables nor chairs, only earthen benches covered with sheep-skins or gay striped blankets. Some of the finer houses enclosed open courts or plazas, in which were trees and shrubs. The cooking was done in the open air, or in round-topped earthen ovens, built outside the houses.

The women washed clothing on flat rocks at the edge of the streams, and young girls carried all the water used for domestic purposes in tall earthen jars borne gracefully on their heads. The beasts of burden were donkeys, or " burros," as the Mexicans call them. Grain was threshed by being laid on smooth earthen threshing-floors, in the open air, and having horses, donkeys, cattle, and sheep driven over it for hours. Wine was kept in skins or great earthen jars. The mountains and hills of the country were covered with pines and cedars, its cultivated valleys with vineyards and fruit orchards; while the raising of flocks and herds was the leading industry of its inhabitants.

At this season of the year, though the sun shone from an unclouded sky of the most brilliant blue, the air was dry and bracing in the daytime, and crisp with the promises of frost at night. It was glorious weather; and, under its influence, the second division ran a line of a

hundred miles down the river in ten days. As
the entire party had looked forward with eager
anticipations to visiting Santa Fé, which is not
on the Rio Grande, but some distance to the east
of it, they were greatly disappointed to be met
by a messenger from General Lyle, with orders
for Mr. Hobart to come into that place, while
his party continued their line south to Albuquerque, eighty miles beyond where they were.

Glen was intensely disappointed at this, for
Santa Fé was one of the places he had been most
anxious to visit. His disappointment was doubled
when Mr. Hobart said that he must take somebody with him as private secretary, and intimated
that his choice would have fallen on the young
front flagman if he had only learned to talk
Spanish. As it was, Binney Gibbs was chosen
for the envied position; for, though he, like the
rest, had only been for a short time among Mexicans, he was already able to speak their language
with comparative ease.

"I don't see how you learned it so quickly,"
said Glen, one day, when, after he had striven in
vain to make a native understand that he wished
to purchase some fruit, Binney had stepped up and
explained matters with a few words of Spanish.

"Why, it is easy enough," replied Binney, "to
anybody who understands Latin."

Then Glen wished that he, too, understood Latin, as he might easily have done as well as his comrade. He wished it ten times more though, when, on acccount of it, Binney rode gayly off to Santa Fé with Mr. Hobart, while he went out to work on the line.

Chapter XXXIII

IN THE VALLEY OF THE RIO GRANDE.

Near the close of a mellow autumn day Glen and "Billy" Brackett sat on a fragment of broken wall and gazed with interest on the scene about them. On one side, crowning a low bluff that overlooked the Rio Grande twelve miles below Albuquerque, was the Indian pueblo of Isletta, a picturesque collection of adobe buildings and stockaded corrals, containing some eight hundred inhabitants. On the other side were extensive vineyards; beyond them were vast plains, from which flocks of bleating sheep were being driven in for the night by Indian boys; and still beyond rose the blue range of the Sierra Madre. The air was so clear and still that through it the sounds of children's voices, the barking of dogs, the bleating of sheep, the lowing of cattle, and the cracked tones of the bell in the quaint old mission church came to the ears of Glen and his companion with wonderful distinctness. The Indian women were preparing their evening meals, and the fragrance of burning cedar drifted down from the village.　Never afterwards could Glen smell the odor of cedar without having the scene of that evening vividly recalled to his mind.

Mingled with this fragrance was another, equally distinct and suggestive.　It was that of crushed grapes; and the two explorers were watching curiously the process of New Mexican wine-making, going on but a short distance from them.　Clumsy ox-carts, constructed without the use of iron, and having great wooden wheels that screeched as they turned on their ungreased wooden axles, brought in loads of purple grapes from the vineyards.　On top of the loads, as though the grapes were so much hay, rode Indian men or boys, armed with wooden pitchforks.　With these they flung the grapes into a great vat of green ox-hides, supported, about ten feet from the ground, by four heavy posts.　The sides of this vat were drawn to a point at the bottom, where there was a small outlet left, through which the grape-juice might flow into a second vat, placed directly beneath the other.　It was similar in all respects to the first, except that it offered no opening for the escape of its contents.

When a load of grapes had been pitched into the upper vat, two naked Indians clambered up, and, springing on top of them, began to tread them with their feet.　For hours they continued this performance, while a steady stream of blood-red juice flowed from the upper vat into the lower. From there it was dipped into huge earthen jars, and set away to ferment.

"Well," said 'Billy' Brackett, at length, as he rose and started towards camp, "I've seen all the native wine-making I want to. If those beggars had only washed themselves first it wouldn't be so bad, but I honestly believe they only take a bath once a year, and that is in grape-juice."

"It is pretty bad," laughed Glen, "though I don't know as it is any worse than their milking." This was a sore point with him, for he was very fond of fresh milk; but, after once witnessing a New Mexican milking, and seeing cows, mares, asses, sheep, and goats all milked into the same vessel, he preferred to go without it.

It was surprising to see what a tall, broad-shouldered fellow Glen was getting to be; and a single glance was sufficient to show what crossing the Plains had done for him. His eyes had the clear look of perfect health; his face, neck, and hands were as brown as sun and wind could make them, while his hair had entirely recovered from its Kansas City shearing, and was now plainly visible beneath the broad sombrero that replaced the hat lost on the Spanish Peak. A heavy blue flannel shirt, a pair of army trousers tucked into the tops of cowhide boots, a leather belt supporting a revolver and a sheath-knife, and a silk handkerchief loosely knotted about his neck, completed his costume.

"Billy" Brackett was dressed in a similar fashion, except that he still clung fondly to the shiny cutaway coat in which he was introduced to the reader, and to which he was deeply attached.

As they walked towards camp, he and Glen discussed the topic now uppermost in their minds, namely, that of their future movements. Since going to Santa Fé, Mr. Hobart had not rejoined them, though a note received from him at Albuquerque promised that he would do so at Isletta, to which place he ordered the line to be run. Now they had been for two days at the Pueblo, but where they were to go next, or whether they were to go any farther, they did not know, and were anxious to find out. They had heard vague rumors that General Lyle was to return to the States, and that all the plans of the expedition might be changed. Thus, when Mr. Hobart galloped into camp just after supper that evening, he was heartily welcomed.

"Where is Binney Gibbs?" was the first question asked.

"Promoted to be private secretary to General Elting, the new chief," was the reply.

"Where is General Elting?"

"He is still in Santa Fé, but is going across with the other two divisions by the Gila route."

"And where are we going?"

"Going to run a one-thousand-mile line from here to the Pacific Ocean, in just the shortest time we can accomplish it."

"Good enough! Hurrah for the Pacific! Hurrah for California!" shouted every member of the party but one. He was the leveller; and when Mr. Hobart, after explaining the dangers and hardships of the trip before them, said that anybody who did not care to encounter them would be furnished with free transportation from that point back to the States, this man decided to accept the offer.

Little did Glen Eddy imagine, as he bade him good-bye the next day, what an effect upon his future the decision thus suddenly reached by the leveller was to have. In the stage from Santa Fé the latter met a gentleman and his wife who were greatly interested in his description of the explorations in which he had just taken part. Among other things, he described Glen Eddy Matherson's remarkable adventures; and the lady, who seemed struck by the boy's name, asked many questions concerning him. Fortunately, the leveller was able to answer most of them, and thus she learned, what Glen had never attempted to conceal, that he was an adopted son of Luke Matherson, of Brimfield, Pennsylvania, who had saved him from a railroad wreck in Glen Eddy creek when he was a baby. She did not explain why she asked these questions, and soon changed the conversation to other topics.

The most immediate effect upon Glen of the leveller's departure was to promote him and increase his pay. As it was impossible, in that country, to engage men of experience to fill places in an engineer corps, Mr. Brackett was obliged to take the level, while Mr. Hobart himself took charge of the transit; and, when the former was asked who he would like as rodman in place of Binney Gibbs, he promptly answered, "Glen Matherson."

In speaking to Glen of this change of position, the division engineer asked the boy if he was sure he wanted to go through to the Pacific.

"Of course I do, sir!" answered Glen, in surprise at the question.

"It is going to be a trip full of danger and all sorts of hardships, possibly including starvation and freezing. I don't know but what you really ought to go back."

"Oh, sir, please don't send me back!" pleaded Glen, earnestly. "I should feel awfully to

have to go home with the trip only half finished."

"Then you are willing to face all the hardships?"

"Yes, sir, I'm willing to face anything, rather
than going back."

"All right!" laughed Mr. Hobart; "I suppose
I shall have to take you along. I proposed to
the general to take Binney Gibbs with him, or
else send him back to the States, because I did
not consider him strong enough to endure what
is ahead of us; but I don't see how I could urge
that in your case, for I actually believe you are
one of the toughest among us."

How Glen rejoiced in his strength as he heard
this! Perhaps it was going to prove as valuable
to him as a scholarship, after all.

"Mr. Brackett is going to run the level, and
wants you for his rodman," continued Mr. Hobart. "The pay will be double what you are
now receiving, and you can soon fit yourself for
the position by a little hard study; for Mr. Brackett is a capital instructor. I have told him that
he may take you on trial, and see what he can
do with you. I also told him of your aversion
to study, and gave him to understand what a
difficult job he had undertaken."

Glen flushed at this, and gazed at the ground

for a moment. Finally he said, "Studying seems very different when you can look right ahead and see what good it is going to do."

"Yes," replied Mr. Hobart, "I know it does. Still, in most cases we have to trust the word of those who can look ahead when we can't. I've no doubt but what you were told at school that a knowledge of Latin would aid you in learning many other languages; but you were not willing to believe it until you saw for yourself how it helped Binney Gibbs pick up Spanish."

Glen did not make any promises aloud in regard to fitting himself for his new position, for he believed in actions rather than words; but he made one to himself, and determined to keep it.

They remained in camp at Isletta one day longer, to prepare for their arduous undertaking, and to engage several new axemen to fill the places of those who had been promoted; but on the second morning the transit was set up over the last stake they had driven, and its telescope was pointed due west.

At first Glen missed the excitement of riding in advance of the party with the front flag. On a preliminary survey, the level can hardly keep up with the transit; and it was not so pleasant to be always behind, striving to catch up, as it had been to be in the lead.

To "Billy" Brackett the change of positions came even harder than to Glen, because in taking the level he had gone back a step rather than forward; but he never showed it. Indeed, by his steady cheerfulness and unceasing flow of good spirits the new leveller soon banished even a shadow of regret from the mind of his young rodman, and taught him to feel a real interest in his new work.

So they slowly climbed the western slope of the Rio Grande Valley, crossed the barren plateau of the divide between it and the Rio Puerco, followed that stream and its tributary, the San José, on the banks of which they saw the ancient pueblos of Laguna and Acoma, into another region of rugged mountains, and, in about two weeks, found themselves at the forlorn frontier post of Fort Wingate, where they were to obtain their final supplies for the winter.

Chapter XXXIV.

BAITING A WOLF-TRAP.

At Fort Wingate the real hardships of the trip began in an unexpected manner. Instead of being plentifully supplied with provisions, as had been reported, the post was found to be very poorly provided, and all that could be spared to the engineers were condemned quartermaster's stores. The party must take these or nothing; and when Mr. Hobart left it to his men whether they should accept the damaged stores and push on, or go back to the Rio Grande, they unanimously said, "Go on!" So, for the next two months, they made the best of half-spoiled hams and bacon, hard-tack filled with white worms, and sugar abounding in little black bugs, that fortunately floated on top of the coffee and could be skimmed off.

The men provided themselves with a number of little luxuries at the sutler's—the last store they would see for months—and "Billy" Brackett bought a cheese. This was considered a very queer purchase; but Glen's was queerer still, for it was a small quantity of strychnine. He only procured this after giving assurances that he did not propose to commit suicide and making many promises to be very careful in its use. What he proposed to do with the poison he did not confide to anybody except his friend "Billy" Brackett, who agreed with him that it was a capital plan.

A run of twelve miles from Fort Wingate brought the party to a camp, in a forest of the most stately yellow-pines they had ever seen, beside a great spring of ice-cold water—known as the Agua Fria (cold water). Here, as soon as supper was over, Glen proceeded to put his great plan into execution. The nights were now very cold, and the boy generally woke before morning to find himself shivering beneath his insufficient covering of blankets. Every night, too, since entering the mountains the party had been annoyed by the sneaking visits and unearthly howlings of wolves that hung on the outskirts of the camp from dark to daylight, every now and then making a quick dash through it, if the guard was not watching sharply, and snatching at bits of food or at anything made of leather that lay in their path. So Glen thought he would teach the wolves a lesson, which should at the same time add some of their skins to his bed-clothing; and it was for this purpose he had procured the strychnine.

19

Now, with "Billy" Brackett's help, he dragged out from one of the wagons a gunny-sack, containing some kidneys, lungs, and other refuse animal matter, obtained from the Fort Wingate butcher, and these he smeared with the deadly powder. Then they prepared several torches of pine slivers, and, amid the unanswered questionings of their companions, left camp, carrying the sack of meat between them. Beginning at a point a few rods from the tents, they strewed the poisoned bait for half a mile along the banks of the little stream flowing from the spring. It was an exciting task, for they seemed to hear suspicious sniffs, and the soft pattering of feet on both sides of them; while Glen felt certain that his torchlight was reflected from gleaming eye-balls more than once. So greatly did these things work upon their imaginations that when, as they started back towards camp, their last torch suddenly went out, leaving them in blackest darkness, they both took to their heels, and raced breathlessly for the distant light of the friendly camp-fire. When they reached it, in perfect safety, they burst out laughing in one another's faces, and wondered what they had run from.

Glen was disappointed, as he lay shivering in his blankets that night, not to hear so many wolves as usual, while the few howls that did reach his ears seemed to come from a distance. Still, he comforted himself with the reflection that dead wolves couldn't howl, and doubtless all those that had ventured near the camp had eaten the poisoned meat, and had their howlings effectually silenced.

It seemed to him that he had hardly dropped asleep when he was rudely awakened by being pulled, feet foremost, out of his blankets, under the side of the tent, and into the open air. At the same moment "Billy" Brackett's laughing voice cried, "Come, Glen, here it is broad daylight, and high time we were gathering in our wolves."

Whew! how cold it was! and in what a hurry Glen sprang from the frozen ground, to rush back into the tent for his boots and army overcoat. He had everything else on, for there was very little undressing at night in that party. As for being sleepy, the biting air had awakened him as effectually as a dash of ice-water.

As they left camp, "Billy" Brackett shouted back to one of the Mexican axemen to follow after them, and the man answered that he would be along in a minute. It was light enough, when they reached the place where they had left the first of the poisoned meat, for them to see it if it had been there; but it was not. Neither was there any dead wolf to be found in the vicinity. It was the same along the whole line, where they had scattered their bait. They could neither discover meat nor wolves.

"Hello!" exclaimed "Billy" Brackett softly, as they were about to turn back, "I believe the wolves are cooking their meat;" and with that he pointed to a thin column of blue smoke rising through the trees at some distance farther down the stream.

"Perhaps they are Indians," suggested Glen.

"Perhaps they are. Let's go and find out. We can take a look at them without being seen. Besides, the Indians hereabout are peaceful now."

So they crept cautiously towards the smoke, until at length they were lying flat on the ground, on the edge of a low bank, with their heads hidden in tufts of grass, peering into a small encampment of Indians just below them. They had hardly gained this position when Glen, uttering a cry of horror, sprang down the bank, rushed in among the Indians, and, snatching a piece of meat from the hands of one of them, who was raising it to his mouth, flung it so far away that it was snapped up and swallowed by a lean, wolfish-looking cur, that had not dared venture near the fire.

At Glen's sudden appearance the Indian women and children ran screaming into the bushes, while the men, springing to their feet, surrounded him with angry exclamations and significant handlings of their knives. They received a second surprise, and fell back a little as "Billy" Brackett, who had not at first understood Glen's precipitate action, came rushing down the bank after him, shouting, "Stand back, you villains! If you lay a hand on him, I'll blow the tops of all your heads off!"

At the same time Glen was making all the faces expressive of extreme disgust that he could think of, and saying, as he pointed to a pile of meat lying in a gunny-sack beside the fire:

"*Carne no bueno! Muy mal! No bueno por hombre!*" which was the best Spanish he knew for, "The meat is not good. It is very bad, and not at all good for a man to eat."

But the Indians could not understand. The meat might not be good enough for white men, who were so very particular, but it was good enough for them. The white men had thrown it away and they had found it. They meant to eat it, too, for they were very hungry. Now, if these uninvited guests to their camp would not clear out and let them eat their breakfast in peace, they must suffer the consequences.

This is what they said; but neither Glen nor

" What is the trouble, Mr. Brackett?" he asked hurriedly, in English.

With a few words they made the situation clear to him, and he, in turn, quickly explained to the Indians that these white men had merely tried to save their lives by preventing them from eating poisoned meat.

" Tell them to look at the dog!" cried Glen, pointing to the poor animal that had swallowed the very bit of meat he had snatched from the Indian, and which was evidently dying.

The sight was a powerful argument, worth more than all the words that could have been spoken.

The Indians sullenly returned to their fire and sat down, while our friends, casting many watchful glances over their shoulders as they went, made good their retreat in the direction of their own camp.

" What kind of Indians were they?" asked Glen, of the Mexican, when they had lost sight of their unpleasant acquaintances.

" Navajos," was the answer.

They were indeed a wretched band of the once wealthy and powerful tribe who claimed that whole country as a pasture-land for their countless flocks and herds. For many years they had been hunted and killed, their flocks driven off and their growing crops destroyed wherever found, until now the main body of the tribe was being slowly starved out of existence on a small reservation in Eastern New Mexico. It was so small that no more Indians could be crowded into it, and the miserable remnant, who still lurked in the fastnesses of their own country, despoiled of all means of procuring a livelihood, prowled about like so many hungry dogs, gleaning the offal from white men's camps, and hunted like wild beasts by all whom they were unfortunate enough to meet.

This band had probably followed Mr. Hobart's party for the sake of what might be picked up in their abandoned camps, and had evidently regarded the poisoned meat, discovered that very morning, as a perfect godsend.

"I reckon we'll have to manage somehow to get along without any wolves," said "Billy" Brackett.

"Yes," replied Glen, regretfully, "I suppose we shall."

Ten miles of line were run that day, through the solemn pine forest, and darkness overtook the party on the very summit of the great Continental Divide. They were crossing the Sierra Madre Mountains, through Zuñi Pass. As Glen subtracted the last reading of his rod for the

day from the last height of instrument, and found that it gave an elevation of 7925 feet, he uttered a shout. For weeks the elevations above sea-level had been steadily mounting upward. This one was a foot lower than the last.

"Hurrah!" he cried, "we are on the Pacific Slope."

It was hard to realize that water, on one side of where they stood, would find its way into the Rio Grande, and so on into the Atlantic, while that but a few feet away would flow through the Colorado into the Pacific. The country did not look any different, but it seemed so. They actually seemed to be breathing the air of the mighty sunset ocean, and this one day's run seemed to place the States, and everything eastern, farther behind them than all the rest of their journey. About the camp-fires that evening the conversation was wholly of California and the golden West, and they sprang to their work the next day with an added zeal.

Fifty miles west of this point they came to Zuñi, one of the most picturesque and by far the most interesting of American towns. First, though, a few miles east of Zuñi, they halted beside the magnificent pile of El Moro, or Inscription Rock, that lifted its frowning battlements, like those of some vast Moorish castle, four hundred feet above the plain. Its base is covered, on all sides, with Indian hieroglyphics, Spanish inscriptions, and English names. Curiously, and almost reverently, our explorers bent down the brushwood near its left-hand corner, and searched until they found the most ancient inscription of all:

"Don Joseph de Basconzeles 1526."

There is nothing more, and this is the sole existing record of Don Joseph's having lived and explored this country while Cortez was still occupying the city of Mexico. Where he came from, who he was, what companions he had, and whither he went will never be known; but through all the centuries that have passed since he carved his name on El Moro's base, the great rock has faithfully preserved the record of his presence.

The next inscription was made nearly one hundred years later, and is a Spanish legend that is translated into, "Passed by this place with despatches, April 16, 1606." There is no name signed, and who passed by on that day can never be told. Then follows innumerable names of Spanish dons, captains, bishops, soldiers, and priests, with varying dates that come down as late as the beginning of the present century.

The first English inscription is, "O. R., March

19, 1836." Then came Whipple, in 1853, followed by many other American soldiers and gold-seekers. Now Glen Eddy and "Billy" Brackett added their names beneath those of the others of Mr. Hobart's party. Then they, too, passed on, leaving a new page of history to be preserved by El Moro for the eyes of future generations.

For some hours before reaching Zuñi they could see it crowning the hill that uplifts it conspicuously above the level of the surrounding plain. It was the "Cibola" of the earliest Spanish explorers, the chief of the seven "golden cities" that they believed to exist in that region, and whose alleged riches led them to undertake the conquest of the country. They called it "Cibola" until they reached it. Then they adopted the native name of Zuñi (pronounced *Zoon-ya*), by which it has been known ever since.

The town, or city, contained some twelve hundred inhabitants, and the hill on which it is built slopes gently up from the plain on one side, but falls away in a precipitous bluff to the narrow waters of the Zuñi River on the other.

"Billy" Brackett had read up on this ancient city of Cibola, and had imparted so much of his information to Glen as to arouse a curiosity in the boy's mind regarding the place fully equal to his own. So, as soon as they reached camp, which was on the plain at the foot of the hill, they hurried off to "do" the town.

Chapter XXXVI.

Zuñi, the Home of the Aztecs.

As the leveller and his rodman ascended the slope on which Zuñi is built, they saw that the town reached entirely across it, and seemingly presented a blank wall of irregular heights, containing only two or three low arched openings. A ladder, here and there, reached from the ground to a flat terrace on top of the wall; but evidently the means of entering the place were few, and could readily be made less. Outside of the wall were long ranges of corrals, fenced with poles, set close together, and fixed firmly in the ground. These poles, which were of all lengths, and the tops of ladders projecting everywhere above the roofs of the town, gave the place a peculiarly ragged and novel appearance. Glen wondered at the height of the buildings, most of which were of five or six stories, and what the ladders were for.

Seeing no other way of gaining an entrance, they followed an Indian, who led a burro bearing an immense load of fagots on his back, into

one of the dark arched passages through the wall.
It was just wide enough to admit the laden don-
key, and so low that, as they followed him, they
were obliged to stoop to avoid striking their
heads against its roof. It was so long that it
evidently led beneath an entire block of houses.

Finally they emerged from its darkness into
one of the most novel plazas, or squares, of the
world. It was surrounded by buildings of several
stories in height, but very few of them had any
doors, while the tiny windows of the lower stories
were placed high up, beyond a man's reach. On
the flat roof of the lower house, or first story, a
second house was built; but it was so much narrower than the first as to leave a broad walk on
the roof in front of it. Above this second house
rose a third, fourth, fifth, and often a sixth, each
one narrower than the one beneath it, so that the
whole looked like a gigantic flight of steps.

These houses were built either of adobe or of
stone, plastered over with adobe mud; and nearly all those on the ground floor were entered, as
Robinson Crusoe entered his castle, by climbing
a ladder to the roof, and descending another that
led down through a skylight. Thus, if an enemy
should succeed in forcing his way through the
narrow tunnel into the plaza, the people would
merely retire to their house-tops, draw up their

ladders, and he would find it as hard to get at them as ever.

The upper tiers of houses had doors opening on the roofs of those below them; but ladders were necessary to climb up from one terrace to another, so that they were everywhere the most prominent feature of the place.

There were but few of the inhabitants in the plaza, or in the narrow lanes leading from it to other open squares; but they swarmed on the flat house-tops, and gazed down on our friends as eagerly as the latter gazed up at them. Americans were curiosities to the people of Zuñi in those days.

" Hello !" exclaimed Glen, as they stood in the middle of the plaza, wondering which way they should go. "Here come some white fellows dressed up like Indians. I wonder who they can be ?"

Sure enough, two young men, having white skins, blue eyes, and yellow hair, but wearing the leggings and striped blankets of Indians, entered the square as Glen spoke. He shouted to them, both in English and Mexican, but they only glanced at him in a startled manner, and then, hurriedly climbing the nearest ladder, they joined a group who were curiously inspecting Glen and his companion from a roof.

" Well! that is queer," said the former. " Who do you suppose those chaps are ?"

" I shouldn't be a bit surprised if they were two of the white Indians I have read of," answered " Billy " Brackett; " and, if so, they are the greatest curiosities we'll see in this town."

" I never heard of them," said Glen. " Where did they come from ?"

" That's more than I can tell, or anybody else. All we know is that the earliest Spaniards found a race of white people living among the Pueblo Indians, whom they describe as being exactly like these chaps grinning at us from that roof. In one respect they are a distinct race, as they have never been allowed to marry with the dark-skinned Indians; but in every other respect they are thorough Puebloes, and there is no tradition going back far enough to show that they were ever anything else. I believe that the race is nearly extinct, and that they are now so few in number as to be rarely seen."

In this " Billy " Brackett was correct; for at that time there were but three of those white Indians in Zuñi, two men and a woman.

Before leaving this remarkable town of curious people, Glen discovered that they kept eagles for pets, and were also very fond of snakes, especially rattlesnakes, which they did not hesitate to han-

20

dle freely and even to hold in their mouths. He saw the entire population turn out on the flat roofs of their houses at daybreak, and, facing the east, patiently await the coming of Montezuma, whom they firmly believed would appear some morning in the place of the sun. He heard of, but was not allowed to see, the perpetual fire, lighted by Montezuma, that has been kept burning for ages by a family of priests, set apart and supported by the people for that particular purpose. He saw women grinding corn into fine white meal between two stones, and baking it into delicious thin cakes on another. He saw them weaving blankets, of sheep's wool, so fine that they will hold water for a whole day, and so strong that they will last a long lifetime. He ate some of the white dried peaches and other fruits that these Indians raise in such abundance and prepare with such skill. And what pleased him more than anything else was that, in exchange for two flour-sacks and a small piece of bacon, one of the Indians made him a fine buckskin shirt, very much adorned with fringes, that he wore all the rest of the winter.

It certainly was a most interesting place, and the whole party would gladly have lingered there longer than the three days that could be spared to it. But it was now November, and they must

be beyond the San Francisco Mountains before
the passes were blocked with heavy snows. So
they bade good-bye to Zuñi and New Mexico, and,
taking their way past Jacob's Well, where a fine
spring bubbles up at the bottom of a funnel-shaped
pit, six hundred feet across at the top, and a hundred and fifty feet deep, they entered the little-
known region of Northern Arizona.

For three months they toiled through that wild
country, as lost to the view and knowledge of
white civilization as though they were running
their line through Central Africa. Then they
emerged on the bank of the mighty Colorado,
and, looking across its turbid flood, saw the barren wastes of the Great Colorado Desert; but
they gave a shout of joy at the sight, for, with
all its dreariness of aspect, that was California,
and beyond it lay the Pacific, the goal of their
hopes.

The last three months had been filled with toil,
hardships, and adventure. Although in that time
they saw no white men, nor men of any kind beyond catching occasional glimpses of the stealthy
Apaches, who hung on their trail for weeks, and
with whom they exchanged more than one rifle-
shot, they were never without evidences that
this whole vast country had once been occupied
by a mighty people. Hardly a day passed that

Glen did not hold his rod on the ruined founda-tion-wall of some huge structure of long ago, or stumble over heaps of broken pottery graceful in form and design, or gaze wonderingly at the stone houses of ancient cliff-dwellers perched on ledges now inaccessible, or walk in the dry beds of crumbling aqueducts, or select choice specimens from piles of warlike implements fashioned from shining crystal or milk-white quartz, or, in some way, have his attention called to the fact that he was traversing a country in which had dwelt millions of his kind, who had long since passed away and been forgotten. He had puzzled over miles of hieroglyphic inscriptions and rude pictures, drawn on the smooth black walls of rugged cañons, and learned from them fragmentary tales of ancient battles or of encounters with savage beasts.

Then, too, he had known hunger and thirst and bitter cold. His Christmas dinner, eaten during a short pause from work on the line, had been a bit of spoiled bacon and a couple of wormy hard-tack, with which, in honor of the day, he had his full share of "Billy" Brackett's treasured cheese, brought out at last to grace this feast. Not only were their provisions nearly exhausted at that time, but it was the fifth day on which they had been unable to wash, for want of water. Two weeks before, a wagon had been sent to the mining-camp of Prescott, nearly a hundred miles away, and they had nearly given up all hopes of its safe return. That night it came into camp, and that night, too, they found a number of rock cisterns full of water. In the darkness of that same evening, while hastening from the pool in which he had been bathing, to get his share of the Christmas supper, poor Glen had run plump into a gigantic cactus, and filled his body with its tiny, barbed thorns. Altogether it was a memorable Christmas, and one he will never forget.

On the last night of December they built a gigantic bonfire of whole trees, and welcomed in the new year by the light of its leaping flames.

They had passed through vast tracts of wonderful fertility and beauty, unknown to white men, and through regions abounding in game that they had no time to hunt. From the summit of the Aztec Pass they had gazed, with dismay, over the boundless expanse of the Black Forest, and then had plunged into its dark depths. They had threaded their way through labyrinths of precipitous cañons, the walls of which rose thousands of feet above their heads, and had known of others still more tremendous.

They had waded through the snows of the San Francisco Mountains, and revelled in the warmth and beauty of the superb Val de Chino, where snow and ice are unknown. They had dodged the crashing boulders hurled down on them in Union Pass by the Hualapi Indians, posted on the inaccessible heights far above them. Here they had lost a wagon, crushed to splinters by one of these masses of rock; but no lives had been sacrificed, and their number was still the same as when they left the Rio Grande. Now they were on the bank of the Colorado, with only one desert and one range of mountains yet to cross. These seemed so little, after all they had gone through; and yet that desert alone was two hundred and fifty miles wide. Two hundred and fifty miles of sand, sage-brush, and alkali; the most barren region of country within the limits of the United States. If they could have looked ahead and seen what the crossing of that desert meant, they would have entered upon the undertaking with heavy hearts and but faint hopes of accomplishing it. How fortunate it is that we cannot look ahead and see the trials that await us. We would never dare face them if they should all appear to us at once; while, by meeting them singly, and attacking them one by one, they are overcome with comparative ease.

But neither Glen nor his companions were

thinking of the trials ahead of them as they came in sight of the Colorado River. They were only thinking of those left behind, and what a glorious thing it was to have got thus far along in their tremendous journey. The transit-party had run their line to the river's bank and gone to camp a mile or so below, when the levellers came up, and Glen held his rod, for a final reading, at the water's edge.

He had just noted the figures in his book, and waved an " All right " to " Billy " Brackett, when he was startled by a rush of hoofs and a joyous shout. The next instant a horse was reined sharply up beside him, while its rider was wringing his hand and uttering almost incoherent words of extravagant joy at once more seeing him.

Chapter XXXVII.

A PRACTICAL USE OF TRIGONOMETRY.

It was Binney Gibbs who had come up the river from Fort Yuma several days before, with General Elting, to meet the second division, and guide them to "The Needles," the point at which the line was to cross the Colorado. The other divisions, which had followed the Gila route, and crossed the Colorado at Fort Yuma, where the desert was narrower, had reached the Pacific ere this, and gone on to San Francisco. The hardest task of all, that of running a line over the desert where it was two hundred and fifty miles wide, had been reserved for Mr. Hobart's men, who had proved themselves so capable of enduring and overcoming hardships.

Binney had waited impatiently in camp until the transit-party reached it, expecting to see Glen ride in at its head with the front flag. Then he had borrowed a horse, and set forth to find the boy whom he had once considered his rival, but whom he now regarded as one of his best friends.

After the first exchange of greetings, they

stood and looked at each other curiously. Glen's hair hung on his shoulders, and the braid that bound the brim of his sombrero was worn to a picturesque fringe, matching that of his buckskin shirt. He was broader and browner than ever; and though his face was still smooth and boyish, these last three months had stamped it with a look of resolute energy that Binney noticed at once.

He, too, was brown, though not nearly so tanned as Glen, in spite of the burning suns of the Gila Valley; for his work had kept him under cover as much as Glen's had kept him in the open air. As General Elting's secretary, Binney had spent most of his time in the ambulance, that, fitted up with writing-desk and table, was the chief-engineer's field-office, or in temporary offices established in tents or houses wherever they had halted for more than a day at a time. He had evidently met with barbers along the comparatively well-travelled Gila; while, as compared with Glen's picturesquely ragged costume, his was that of respectable civilization. Although he, too, was the picture of health, his frame lacked the breadth and fulness of Glen's, and it was evident at a glance that, in the matter of physical strength, he was even more greatly the other's inferior than when they left Brimfield.

Glen could not help noting this with a feeling of secret satisfaction; but, as they rode towards camp together, and Binney described his winter's experiences, Glen began to regard him with vastly increased respect. He thought he had studied hard, and done well to master the mysteries of adjusting and running a level, perfecting himself as a rodman, and learning to plot profile; but his knowledge appeared insignificant as compared with that which Binney had picked up and stored away. Not only had he learned to speak Spanish fluently, but he had become enough of a geologist to talk understandingly of coal-seams and ore-beds. He had the whole history of the country through which he had passed, from the date of its Spanish discovery, at his tongue's end. He spoke familiarly of the notable men to whom, at General Elting's dictation, he had written letters, and altogether he appeared to be a self-possessed, well-informed young man of the world.

Poor Glen was beginning to feel very boyish and quite abashed in the presence of so much wisdom, and to wonder if he had not been wasting his opportunities on this trip as he had those of school. His thoughts were inclining towards a decidedly unpleasant turn, when they were suddenly set right again by Binney, who exclaimed,

"But, I say, old man, what a fine thing you fellows have done this winter! The general declares that you have made one of the most notable surveys on record; and it's a thing every one of you ought to be proud of. You should have heard him congratulate Mr. Hobart. He asked at once about you, too, and wants to see you as soon as you get in. He seems to take a great interest in you, and has spoken of you several times. I expect, if you choose to keep on in this business, you can always be sure of a job through him. He seems to think it queer that you should be a year older than I am; but I told him it was certainly so, because I knew just when your birthday came."

Glen was on the point of saying that, if Binney knew that, it was more than he did, but something kept him silent. He hated to acknowledge that he knew nothing of his real birthday, nor how old he really was, but he wondered if he could truly be a year older than this wise young secretary.

At this point the conversation was interrupted by their arrival at camp, and by General Elting stepping from his tent to give Glen a hearty handshake as he exclaimed,

"My dear boy, I am delighted and thankful to see you again. I tried to persuade our friend

Mr. Hobart, when I last saw him at Santa Fé, that, in spite of your performance on that railroad ride you and I took together last summer, you were too young to make the trip I had laid out for him. He said he didn't know anything about your age, but that you were certainly strong and plucky enough for the trip. I made him promise, though, to try and induce you to go back from Isletta; but he doesn't seem to have succeeded."

"No, sir," laughed Glen, "and I'm awfully glad he didn't, for it's been the most glorious kind of a trip, and I have enjoyed every minute of it."

"I am glad, too, now that it is all over; but I must tell you that, if I had not been assured that you were a whole year older than my young secretary here, I should have insisted on your going back, for I considered it too hard and dangerous a trip for a boy so young as I had supposed you to be until then."

Here was another good reason why Glen was glad he had remained silent on the subject of his birthday.

"Now what do you think of running a line across the desert ahead of us?" continued the chief-engineer; "are you as anxious to undertake that as you were to cross Arizona?"

“Yes, indeed, I am, sir,” replied Glen, earnestly. “I am anxious to go wherever the second division goes; and if anybody can get a line across that desert, I know we can.”

“I believe you can,” said the chief, smiling at the boy’s enthusiasm, “and I am going along to see how you do it.”

The Colorado was so broad, deep, and swift that Glen wondered how they were going to measure across it, and had a vague idea that it could be done by stretching a long rope from bank to bank. He asked “Billy” Brackett; and when the leveller answered, “By triangulation, of course,” Glen showed, by his puzzled expression, that he was as much in the dark as ever.

“You have studied geometry and trigonometry, haven’t you?” asked the leveller.

Glen was obliged to confess that, as he had not been able to see the use of those studies, he had not paid much attention to them.

“Well, then, perhaps you’ll have a better opinion of old Euclid when you see the practical use we’ll put him to to-morrow,” laughed “Billy” Brackett.

Glen did see, the next day, and wondered at the simplicity of the operation. The front flag was sent across the river in a boat, and on the opposite side he drove a stake. While he was thus engaged, a line a quarter of a mile long was measured on the bank where the rest of the party still remained, and a stake was driven at each end of it. The transit was set up over one of these stakes, and its telescope was pointed first at the other and then at the one across the river, by which means the angle where it stood was taken. It was then set over the stake at the other end of the measured line, and that angle was also taken. Then Mr. Hobart drew, on a leaf of his transit-book, a triangle, of which the base represented the line measured between the two stakes on his side of the river, and one side represented the distance across the river that he wished to find. He thus had one side and two angles of a triangle given to find one of the other two sides, and he solved the problem as easily as any boy or girl of the trigonometry-class can whose time in school has not been wasted as Glen Eddy's was.

It was a simple operation, and one easily performed, but it involved a knowledge of the four fundamental rules of arithmetic, of proportion, or the rule of three, of geometry, of trigonometry, and of how to use a surveyor's transit; all of which, except the last, are included in the regular course of studies of every boy and girl in America who receives a common-school education.

Glen had also been sent across the river, where he held his rod so high up on the bank that the cross hair in the telescope of the level cut just one tenth of an inch above its bottom. Then, when "Billy" Brackett came over, and went on beyond Glen, he set the level up so high on the bank that, through it, he could just see the top of the rod, extended to its extreme length. So they climbed slowly up out of the Colorado Valley, and began to traverse the dreary country that lay between it and the Sierra Nevada.

For the first hundred miles or so they got along very well, so far as water was concerned, though the mules and horses speedily began to grow thin and weak for want of food. The patches of grass were very few and far between, and the rations of corn exceedingly small; for in that country corn was worth its weight in gold, and scarce at that.

Chapter XXXVIII.

DYING OF THIRST IN THE DESERT.

MATTERS were bad enough by the time Mr. Hobart's party reached Camp Cady, nearly half way across the desert; but, from there on, they became much worse. The line could no longer follow the winding government trail, but must be run straight for the distant mountains, that were now plainly to be seen.

This experience vividly recalled that of the preceding summer, when they were crossing the Plains towards the Rocky Mountains, and longing so eagerly to reach them. But this was infinitely worse than that. There they generally found water that was sweet and fit to drink, and always had plenty of grass for their stock. Here they rarely found water, and when they did it was nearly always so strongly impregnated with salt, soda, and alkali as to be unfit to drink. Here, too, instead of grass, they found only sand, sage brush, greasewood, and cacti. To be sure the greasewood was a comfort, because it burned just as readily green as dry, and in certain of the cacti, round ones covered with long curved spines, they could nearly always find a mouthful of water, but none of these things afforded any nourishment for the hungry animals. They became so ravenous that they gnawed off one another's manes and tails, chewed up the wagon covers, and every other piece of cloth they could get hold of. Then they began to die so fast from starvation and exhaustion that some dead ones were left behind with every camp, and each day the number was increased.

At nearly every camp, too, a wagon was abandoned, and for miles they could look back and see its white cover, looming above the dreary expanse of sand and sage, like a monument to the faithful animals that had fallen beside it. At length but one wagon and the two ambulances were left. Tents, baggage, clothing, all the bedding except one blanket apiece, and the greater part of their provisions, had been thrown away, or left in the abandoned wagons. Within forty miles of the mountains they gave up work on the line. The men had no longer the strength to drag the chain or carry the instruments. They still noted their course by compass, and the height of various elevations as they crossed them, by the barometer. They were even able to measure the distance from one sad camping-place to another, by means of the odometer, an instrument that, attached to a wagon-wheel, records the number of revolutions made by it. This number, multiplied by the circumference of the wheel, gave them the distance in feet and inches. Everybody was now on foot, even the chief's saddle-horse, Señor, and Glen's Nettle being harnessed to one of the ambulances.

At last, when the mountains appeared tantalizingly near, but when they were still nearly twenty miles away, it seemed as though the end had come. For two days neither men nor animals had tasted a drop of water. At the close of the second day, a slight elevation had disclosed a lake lying at their feet, glowing in the red beams of the setting sun. With feeble strength they had rushed to it, and flung themselves into its tempting waters. They were as salt as brine, and, with this bitter disappointment, came despair. They lighted fires and made coffee with the brackish water that oozed into holes dug in the salt-encrusted sand, but it sickened them, and they could not drink it.

Their lips were cracked, their tongues swollen, their throats like dry leather, and their voices were hardly more than husky whispers.

As the moon rose that evening, and poured its cold light on the outstretched forms grouped about the solitary, white-sheeted wagon, a hand was laid on Glen's shoulder, and the chief's voice bade the boy rise and follow him. Leading the way to the ambulance in which Binney Gibbs slept the sleep of utter exhaustion and despair, and to which the horses Señor and Nettle were fastened, the general said,

"There is but one hope left for us, Matherson. It is certain that some of the party have not strength enough to carry them to the mountains, and equally so that, without water, the teams can never reach there. In the valleys of these mountains are streams, and on these streams are ranches. If we can get word to one of these, the entire party may yet be saved. I am going to try and ride there to-night, and I want you to come with me. Our horses, and yours in particular, are the freshest of all the animals. I have told Mr. Hobart; but there is no need of rousing any of the others to a sense of their misery. Will you make the attempt with me?"

Of course the boy would go; and, for a moment, he almost forgot his sufferings, in a feeling of pride that he should be selected for such an undertaking.

A minute later they rode slowly away, and the desert sands so muffled the sound of their horses' hoofs that their departure was not noted by those whom they left.

With fresh, strong animals, and without that terrible choking thirst, that night ride over the moonlight plain would have been a rare pleasure. Under the circumstances it was like a frightful dream. Neither of the riders cared to talk; the effort was too painful; but both thought of the last ride they had taken together in the cab of a locomotive on a Missouri railroad, and the man looked tenderly at the boy, as he recalled the incidents of that night. For an hour they rode in silence, their panting steeds maintaining a shambling gait through the sand, that was neither a trot nor a lope, but a mixture of the two. Then they dropped into a walk, and, for another hour, were only roused to greater speed by infinite exertions on the part of their riders. At last Señor stumbled heavily, recovered himself, and then fell.

"There is no use trying to get him up again," said the chief. "I'm afraid the poor old horse is done for; but you must ride on, and I will follow on foot. Head for that dark space. It marks a valley. I shall not be far behind you. If you find water, fire your pistol. The sound will give me new strength. Good-bye, and may God prosper you."

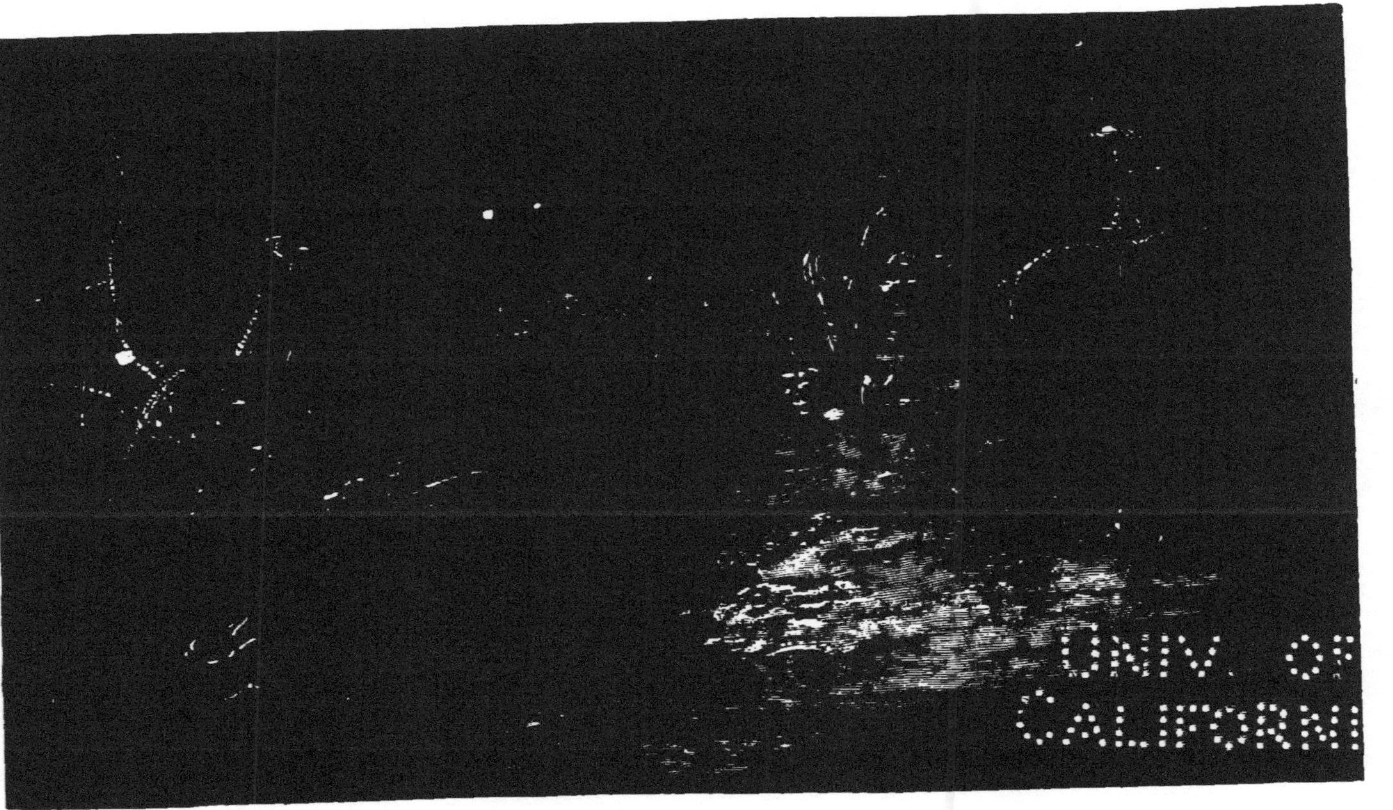

"'HEAD FOR THAT DARK SPACE. IT MARKS A VALLEY. . . . IF YOU FIND WATER, FIRE YOUR PISTOL.'"

“ But I hate to leave you, sir.”

“ Never mind me ; hurry on. A moment wasted now may be at the price of a life.”

So Glen went on alone, trying, in husky tones, to encourage his brave little mare, and urge her to renewed efforts. She seemed to realize that this was a struggle for life, and responded nobly. She even broke into a lope, as the ground became harder. The sand was disappearing. Water might be nearer than they thought.

Five miles farther Nettle carried her rider, and then she staggered beneath his weight. She could not bear him a rod farther, and he knew it. A choking sob rose in the boy’s parched throat as he dismounted and left her standing there, the plucky steed that had brought him so far and so faithfully ; but he could not stay with her, he must go on. He could see the opening to the valley plainly now, though it was still some miles away ; and, summoning all his strength, he walked towards it.

At half the distance he was skirting a foot-hill, when down its gravelly side, directly towards him, rushed two animals, like great dogs. They were mountain-wolves at play, one chasing the other, and they came on, apparently without seeing him. When, with a hoarse cry, he attracted their attention, they stopped, and, sitting on their haunches, not more than a couple of rods away, gazed at him curiously.

He dared not fire at them, for fear of only wounding one and thus arousing their fury. Nor did he wish to raise false hopes in the mind of General Elting, who might hear the shot and think it meant water.

Some one had told him of the cowardice of wolves. He would try it. Picking up a stone, he flung it at them, at the same time running forward, brandishing his arms, and giving a feeble shout. They sprang aside, hesitated a moment, and then turned tail and fled.

Soon afterwards Glen reached the valley, which was apparently about half a mile broad. On its farther side was a line of shadow blacker than the rest. It might be timber. With tottering footsteps the boy staggered towards it. As his feet touched a patch of grass he could have knelt and kissed it, but at the same instant he heard the most blessed sound on earth, the trickling of a rivulet. He fell as he reached it, and plunged his head into the life-giving water. It was warm and strongly impregnated with sulphur; but never had he tasted anything so delicious, nor will he ever again.

Had it been cold water, the amount that he drank might have killed him; as it was, it only made him sick. After a while he recovered, and then how he gloated in that tiny stream. How he bathed his hands and face, and, suddenly, how he wished the others were there with him. Perhaps a shot might bear the joyful news to the ears of the general.

With the thought he drew his revolver, and roused the mountain echoes with its six shots, fired in quick succession. Then he tried to walk up the valley in the hope of finding a ranch. It was all he could do to keep on his feet, and only a mighty effort of will restrained him from flinging himself down on the grass and going to sleep beside that stream of blessed water.

A few minutes later there came a quick rush of hoofs from up the valley, and in the moonlight he saw two horsemen galloping towards him. They dashed up with hurried questions as to the firing they had heard, and, somehow, he managed to make them understand that a party of white men were dying of thirst twenty miles out on the desert.

The next thing he knew, he was in a house, and dropping into a sleep of such utter weariness that to do anything else would have been beyond his utmost power of mind or body.

Chapter XXXIX.

CROSSING THE SIERRA NEVADA.

WHEN Glen next woke to a realizing sense of his surroundings, the evening shadows had again fallen, and he heard familiar voices near by him. All were there, General Elting, Mr. Hobart, "Billy" Brackett, Binney Gibbs, and the rest, just sitting down to a supper at the hospitable ranch table. It was laden with fresh beef, soft bread, butter, eggs, milk, boiled cabbage, and tea, all of them luxuries that they had not tasted for months. And they had plates, cups and saucers, spoons, knives, and forks. Glen wondered if he should know how to use them; but he did not wonder if he were hungry. Nor did he wait for an invitation to join that supper-party.

He was dirty and ragged and unkempt as he entered the room in which his comrades were assembled; but what did they care? He was the one who had found help and sent it to them in the time of their sore need. Some of them owed their lives to him, perhaps all of them did. Every man in the room stood up, as the chief took him by the hand and led him to the head of the table, saying,

"Here he is, gentlemen. Here is the lad who saved the second division. Some of us might have got through without his help; others certainly would not. Right here I wish to thank him, and to thank God for the strength, pluck, and powers of endurance with which this boy, to whom we owe so much, is endowed."

And Glen! How did he take all this praise? Why, he was so hungry, and his eyes were fixed so eagerly on the table full of good things spread before him that he hardly knew what the general was talking about. If they would only let him sit down and eat, and drink some of that delicious-looking water! He came very near interrupting the proceedings by doing so. At length, to his great relief, they all sat down, and in a moment Glen was eating and drinking in a manner only possible to a hearty boy who has gone without water and almost without food for two days.

A little later, seated before a glorious camp-fire of oak logs outside the ranch, Glen learned how the two ranchmen, after getting him to the house, had loaded a wagon with barrels of water and gone out on the desert. They first found General Elting, nearly exhausted, but still walking, within a couple of miles of the valley, and afterwards discovered the rest of the party dragging themselves falteringly along beside one of the ambulances, which, with the notes and maps of the expedition, was the only thing they had attempted to bring in.

And Nettle! Oh, yes; the brave little mare was also found, revived, and brought in to the ranch. She needed a long rest; and both for her sake and as a token of his gratitude, Glen presented her to one of the ranchmen. The settlers went out that same night after the other ambulance and the wagon, abandoned on the shore of the salt lake. When they returned, General Elting traded his big, nearly exhausted army mules for their wiry little bronchos, giving two for one, and thus securing fresh teams to haul all that remained of his wagon-train to the coast.

The party spent three days in recruiting at this kindly ranch, to which they will always look back with grateful hearts, and think of as one of the most beautiful spots on earth. Then, strengthened and refreshed, they passed on up the valley, which proved to be that of the Tehachapa, the very pass towards which they had directed their course from the moment of leaving the Colorado.

How beautiful seemed its oak-groves, its mead.
ows, its abounding springs of cool, sweet water,
and its clear, bracing air! How they ate and
slept and worked and enjoyed living! What
grand camp-fires they had, and how much merriment circulated about them! And had they not
cause for rejoicing? Had they not toiled across
half the width of a continent? Had they not
traversed vast plains and mountain-ranges and
deserts? Had they not encountered savage men
and savage beasts? Had they not suffered from
hunger, thirst, cold, and hardships of all kinds?
Had they not conquered and triumphed over all
these? Were they not left far behind, and was
not the journey's end in sight? No wonder they
were light-hearted and excited, and no wonder
they seemed to inhale champagne with every
breath of that mountain air!

General Elting left them at the summit of the
pass, and, taking Binney Gibbs with him in his
private ambulance, hastened on to Los Angeles
to make arrangements for the transportation of
the party, by steamer, up the coast to San Francisco; for there were no railroads in California
in those days.

The rest of the engineers travelled leisurely
down the western slope of the Sierras into a region that became more charming with each mile

of progress. It was spring-time. The rainy season was drawing to its close, and the Golden State was at its best. The air was filled with the sweet scents of innumerable flowers, the song of birds, and the music of rushing waters. The bay-trees wore their new spring robes of vivid green, from which the soft winds shook out delightfully spicy odors. The trunks of the manzanitas glowed beneath their wine-red skins, while the madronos were clad in glossy, fawn-colored satins. To the toil-worn explorers, just off the alkaline sands of the parched and verdureless desert, the old mission of San Gabriel, nestled at the base of the western foot-hills, seemed the very garden-spot of the world. Here were groves of oranges, lemons, limes, pomegranates, and olives. Here were roses and jasmines. Here were heliotrope and fuchsias, grown to be trees, and a bewildering profusion of climbing vines and flowering shrubs, of which they knew not the names.

But they recognized the oranges, though none of them had ever seen one growing before; and, with a shout of joy, the entire party rushed into the grove, where the trees were laden at once with the luscious fruit and perfumed blossoms. There was no pause to discuss the proper method of peeling an orange in this case, for they did not stop to peel them at all. They just ate them, skin and all, like so many apples. It was such a treat as they had never enjoyed before, and they made the most of it.

Not long after leaving San Gabriel, as they were making a night march towards Los Angeles, Glen suddenly became aware of a strange humming sound above his head; and, looking up, saw a telegraph wire. With a glad shout he announced its presence. It was the most civilized thing they had seen since leaving Kansas.

At Los Angeles they could not make up their minds to endure the close, dark rooms of the Fonda, and so camped out for the night in the government corral beside their wagon.

The following day they made their last march over twenty miles of level prairie, dotted with flocks and herds, to San Pedro, on the coast. It was late in the afternoon, and the sun was setting, when, from a slight eminence, they caught their first glimpse of the gold-tinted Pacific waters. For a moment they gazed in silence, with hearts too full for words. Then everybody shook hands with the one nearest to him, and more than one tear of joyful emotion trickled down the bronzed and weather-beaten cheeks of the explorers. As for Glen Eddy, he never expects to be so thrilled again as he was by the sight of that mighty ocean gleaming in the red light of the setting sun, and marking the end of the most notable journey of his life.

That night they made their last camp, and gathered about their final camp-fire. Glen and "Billy" Brackett had shared their blankets ever since leaving the Rio Grande, and had hardly slept, even beneath a canvas roof, in all those months. Now, as they lay together for the last time, on their bed of grassy turf, which is of all beds the one that brings the sweetest and soundest sleep, and gazed at the stars that had kept faithful watch above them for so long, they talked in low tones until a gentle sea-breeze set in and they were lulled to sleep by the murmur of distant breakers, a music now heard by both of them for the first time in their lives.

The next day they turned over their sole remaining wagon and their ambulance to a government quartermaster. Then, having no baggage, they were ready, without further preparation, to embark on the steamer *Orizaba* for San Francisco, to which place General Elting and Binney Gibbs had gone on, by stage, from Los Angeles, some days before.

As the great ship entered the Golden Gate and steamed up the bay, past Tamalpias, past the Presidio, past Alcatraz Island, and into the harbor of San Francisco, Glen Eddy found it hard to realize that it was all true, and that this young explorer, who was about to set foot in the city of his most romantic day dreams, was really the boy who had started from Brimfield ten months before, without an idea of what was before him.

CHAPTER XL

A HOME AND TWO FATHERS.

OF course they all went to the Occidental, for everybody went first to the Occidental in those days. As they drove through the city, in open carriages, their long hair, buckskin shirts, rags, in some cases soleless and toeless boots, and generally wild and disreputable appearance attracted much amused attention from the well-dressed shoppers of Montgomery Street; and, when they trooped into the marble rotunda of the great hotel, they excited the universal curiosity of its other and more civilized guests.

But they did not mind—they enjoyed the sensation they were creating; and Glen, who was one of the wildest-looking of them all, rather pitied Binney Gibbs on account of the fine clothing he had already assumed, as the two met and exchanged hearty greetings once more.

"Come up into my room, Glen," said Binney, eagerly, "I've got a lot of Brimfield news, and there's a pile of letters for you besides. Only think, Lame Wolf is playing short-stop on the ball nine, and they say he's going to make one of the best players they've ever had."

The last news Glen had received from home was in the letters Mr. Hobart had brought from Santa Fé nearly five months before. He had learned then of Lame Wolf's safe arrival at Brimfield, and of his beginning to study English; but now to hear of his being on the ball nine! That was making progress; and the boy felt very proud of his young Indian. But there was more startling news than that awaiting him. In one of the letters from his adopted father, which, though it bore the latest date, had already been waiting in San Francisco more than a month, he read, with amazement, the following paragraphs:

"I have just received a note from a lady who writes that she met a gentleman in New Mexico who told her all about you. She was intensely interested, because she thinks she knew your mother, and travelled with her and you on the day the train was wrecked in Glen Eddy creek, when you and I were the only survivors. She also says that the mother with whom she travelled said her baby was just a year old, and that day was his birthday. So, my dear boy, if it should happen that you and the baby she mentions are the same, you are a year younger than we have always thought you, and are just the age of Binney Gibbs.   In conclusion, the lady writes that she believes your real father to be still alive, and she thinks she knows his name, but prefers not to mention it until she hears from me all that I know of your history.   I, of course, wrote to her at once, and am anxiously expecting an answer.   I never loved you more than now, and to give you up will well-nigh break my heart; but, if there is anything better in store for you than I can offer, I would be the last one to stand in the way of your accepting it.

"Now, my dear boy, come home as soon as you can, and perhaps you will find two fathers awaiting you instead of one.   We are full of anxiety concerning you.   Be sure and telegraph the moment you arrive in San Francisco."

Over and over did Glen read this letter before he could control himself sufficiently to speak. Binney Gibbs noticed his agitation, and finally said,

"No bad news, I hope, old man?"

For answer the boy handed him the letter, which Binney read with ever-growing excitement.   When he finished he exclaimed, "It's wonderful, Glen, and I do hope it will come out all right.   I always felt sorry for you at not knowing who you were, even when I was so meanly jealous of you for being stronger and more popular than I, and now I congratulate you from the bottom of my heart. What a lucky thing it has been though, over and over again, not only for you, but for me, and the whole second division, that you were stronger than I!" he added, with a hearty sincerity that he would not have exhibited a year before. "I tell you what, this trip has opened my eyes to some things, and one of them is that a fellow's body needs just as much training as his mind."

"It has opened mine too," said Glen, earnestly. "It has taught me that, no matter how strong a fellow is, he can't expect to amount to much in this world unless he knows something, and that he can't know much unless he learns it by hard study. If ever I get a chance to go to school again, you better believe I'll know how to value it."

"And if I ever get another chance to learn how to swim, you may be sure I won't throw it away in a hurry," laughed Binney.

"Only see what a splendid fellow 'Billy' Brackett is," continued Glen, "just because he has trained his muscle and his brain at the same time, without letting either get ahead of the other. And, speaking of 'Billy' Brackett, I must go and show him this letter, because he is one of the best friends I have got in the world, and I know he'll be glad to hear anything that pleases me."

First, Glen stopped at the telegraph office in the hotel, and sent the following despatch to Brimfield.

" Just arrived, safe and sound. Start for home first steamer," for which he paid eight dollars in gold.

Then he went to "Billy" Brackett's room, where he found that young engineer struggling with a new coat that had just been sent in from a tailor's, and lamenting, more than ever, the loss of his shiny but well-loved old cutaway that had been eaten by one of the hungry mules on the desert.

He was as interested as Glen knew he would be in the letter, and as he finished it he exclaimed :

" Well, you are in luck, my boy, and I'm glad of it ! Here I am, without a father to my name, while you seem likely to have two. Well, you deserve a dozen ; and if you had 'em, each one would be prouder of you than the other."

After a week spent in San Francisco, during which time the barber, tailor, and various outfitters made a marvellous change in Glen's personal appearance, he, together with General El-

ting and Binney Gibbs, boarded one of the great
Pacific Mail Steamships for Panama. Mr. Hobart, "Billy" Brackett, and the other members
of the second division, had decided to remain for
a while on that coast, and most of them had already accepted positions on some of the various
engineering works then in progress in California; but they were all at the steamer to see the
homeward-bound travellers off. As the great
wheels were set in motion, and the stately ship
moved slowly from the wharf, the quieter spectators were startled by the tremendous farewell
cheer that arose from the "campmates" who remained behind; and the cries of "good-bye, general! we'll be on hand whenever you want us
again! Good-bye, Grip! Good-bye, Glen, old
man! We won't forget the desert in a hurry!
Good-bye!"

The run down the coast was a smooth and
pleasant one; while the several Mexican and
Central American ports at which they touched
were full of interest and delightful novelty to the
Brimfield boys. They thoroughly enjoyed crossing the Isthmus, and would gladly have lingered
longer amid its wonderful tropic scenery. Not
until they were on the Atlantic, however, and
steaming northward, did they realize that they
were fairly on their way home.

One day, as the two boys were sitting on deck, in company with General Elting, gazing at the coast of Cuba, which they were then passing, Binney Gibbs broke a long silence with the remark, " Doesn't it seem queer, Glen, to think that when you get home you will be just the age you were when you left it, and perhaps your name won't be ' Glen Eddy' after all ?"

General Elting had not heard of Glen's letter from his adopted father, nor had he ever heard him called " Glen Eddy " before; and now he asked Binney what he meant by such a curious speech.

When it was explained, he sat silent for several minutes, looking at Glen with such a peculiar expression that the boy grew uneasy beneath the fixed gaze. Then, without a word, he rose and walked away, nor did they see him again for several hours. He talked much with Glen during the remainder of the voyage, and frequently puzzled him by his questions, and the interest he manifested in everything relating to his past life.

As he was going to St. Louis, he took the same train with the boys from New York ; and, though he bade them good-bye as they neared Brimfield, he said that he hoped and expected to see them again very shortly.

How natural the place looked as the train

rolled up to the little station, and how impossible it was to realize that they had crossed the continent and sailed on two oceans since leaving it!

"There's father!" shouted Glen and Binney at the same instant.

"And there are all the boys! Who is that dark, good-looking chap with them? It can't be Lame Wolf! But it is, though! Did you ever see such a change for the better? Bully for Lame Wolf!"

"Hurrah for Glen Eddy! Hurrah for Binney Gibbs!" shouted the Brimfield boys, wild with the excitement of welcoming home two such heroes as the young explorers were in their eyes. The very first to grasp Glen's hand was the Indian lad, and he said in good English, though with a Cheyenne accent, "How Glen! Lem Wolf is very glad. Lem Wolf is short-stop now. He can play ball."

Binney Gibbs disappeared in his father's carriage; but Glen walked from the station with his adopted father, and everybody wanted to shake hands with him, and ask him questions, and throng about him, so that it seemed as though they never would reach home.

It was a happy home-coming, and Glen was touched by the interest and the kindly feeling manifested towards him; but how he did long to reach the house, and be alone for a minute with Mr. Matherson. There was one question that he was so eager, and yet almost afraid, to ask. Had his own father been discovered? But he could not ask it before all those people, nor did he have an opportunity for a full hour after they reached the house. Some of the neighbors were there, and they had to have supper, and everything seemed to interfere to postpone that quiet talk for which he was so anxious.

At length he could wait no longer, and, almost dragging Mr. Matherson into the little front parlor, he closed the door and said breathlessly, "Now tell me, father; tell me quick! Is he alive? Have you found him?"

" Yes, my boy, he is alive, or was a few months ago, and I think we can find him. In fact, I believe you know him very well, and could tell me where to find him better than I can tell you."

"What do you mean?" cried Glen. "Oh, tell me quick! What is his name?"

There was so much confusion outside that they did not notice the opening of the front gate, nor the strange step on the walk. As Mr. Matherson was about to reply to the boy's eager question, the parlor door opened, and one of the children entered, with a card in her hand, saying,

"Somebody wants to see you, papa."

As Mr. Matherson glanced at the card he sprang to his feet, trembling with excitement.

"Gerald Elting!" he cried. "Why, Glen, that is the name of your own father!"

"And here is his own father, eager to claim his son," came from the open doorway, in the manly tones that Glen had long since learned to love.

The next moment the man's arms were about the boy's neck, as, in a voice trembling with long-suppressed emotion, he cried,

"Oh, my son, my son! Have I found you after all these years? Now is my long sorrow indeed turned to joy."

THE END.